The Girls of Cincinnati

"A literary gem... sizzling thriller!"

by

JACK ENGELHARD

DayRay Literary Press
British Columbia, Canada

The Girls of Cincinnati

Copyright ©2009, 2014 by Jack Engelhard
ISBN-13 978-1-77143-139-2
Second Edition

Library and Archives Canada Cataloguing in Publication
Engelhard, Jack, 1940-, author
The girls of Cincinnati / by Jack Engelhard. – Second edition.
Issued in print and electronic formats.
ISBN 978-1-77143-139-2 (pbk.).--ISBN 978-1-77143-140-8 (pdf)
Additional cataloguing data available from Library and Archives Canada

Jack Engelhard may be contacted through: **www.jackengelhard.com**

Cover artwork: Slender female legs in a long skirt © Oksvik | CanStockPhoto.com

Previously published in 2009 by CreateSpace.

DayRay Literary Press is a literary imprint
of CCB Publishing: www.ccbpublishing.com

DayRay Literary Press
British Columbia, Canada
www.dayraypress.com

The Girls of Cincinnati

Pure Engelhard gem. In this one, _The Girls of Cincinnati_, he's given us something never thought possible, a coming-of-age saga that's also a sizzling thriller. The plot here is riveting. The dialogue sparkles. What's it about? It's about life. Anyone who's been in love - especially love that appears to be out of reach - will understand what's going on between Engelhard's two heroes, Eli Brilliant and Stephanie Eaton. Anyone who feels the approach of menace will understand what these two must endure when a crazed woman appears on the scene, threatening them both with "a fate worse than death."

Anyone who works at a dead-end job will be right there with Eli, who ends up working for Harry's Carpet City in Cincinnati, Ohio. Eli is back home in the Midwest after he failed to make it in New York as an actor. So that's one dream down the drain. But now that he's back in Cincinnati, he's got Stephanie Eaton - or does he? Something always goes wrong between them, and this time, terribly wrong.

Engelhard, the last of the Hemingways, gives us the heartland of America as it's rarely been given to us before in literature. He gives us an unvarnished view inside the world of Sales and he gives us a broken-down old salesman that's the equal of anything produced by Arthur Miller and

David Mamet. Engelhard is most precious in his asides, his quick-cut commentaries.

In Eli Brilliant, Engelhard gives us a character, though young and handsome, who we can all identify with - especially when we find Eli always reaching for the unattainable. Yes, he's a lover, a chick magnet - hence the title - but don't be fooled. This character, and this novel, goes much deeper.

From start to finish, *The Girls of Cincinnati* is a triumph.

Praise received for *The Girls of Cincinnati*

"A literary gem! I could not put it down."
- John W. Cassell, author of *Crossroads: 1969*

"Engelhard tells the story of *The Girls of Cincinnati* with precision through his masterful narration. Every word has a place and every page has a quote you will want to remember."
- Lois Sack, author of *Her Brightness in the Darkness*

A Note from the Author

This – *The Girls of Cincinnati* – is the first novel I ever wrote and I kept it in reserve all these years because first love comes around only once. I finally decided to let it go when it became obvious that I wasn't getting any younger. Once your work gets published it's no longer your secret. Over the years (decades actually) I kept polishing it, nursing it and nourishing it, always mindful that I mustn't tamper too much, otherwise I'd lose the innocence, the youthfulness and even the heartbreak in which it was first written. We never want to get too sophisticated. I began writing it in New Jersey after departing Cincinnati for good, and leaving behind so many people that I knew, and one or two that I even loved.

JE

Also by Jack Engelhard

Indecent Proposal: Fiction.
Translated into more than 22 languages and turned into a Paramount motion picture of the same name starring Robert Redford and Demi Moore.

Compulsive: A Novel: Fiction.

Escape From Mount Moriah: Memoir.
Award-winner for writing and film.

The Days of the Bitter End: Fiction.

Slot Attendant: A Novel About A Novelist: Fiction.

The Prince of Dice: Fiction.

The Bathsheba Deadline: Fiction.

The Horsemen: Non-fiction.
Excerpted in *The New York Times*

* * * * *

A new Spanish language edition of *Indecent Proposal* was released in 2013 in both print and e-book editions and made available for purchase worldwide.

The author wishes to express his gratitude and thanks to translator Frederick Martin-Del-Campo for his fine work in this and other projects.

"Precise, almost clinical language...Is this book fun to read? You betcha."
- *The New York Times,* for *Indecent Proposal*

"Well-wrought characters, exhilarating pace...funny and gruff...a fast and well-crafted book."
- *Philadelphia Inquirer,* for *Indecent Proposal*

"*Compulsive* is enormously enjoyable, and so easy to get into."
- Kenneth Slawenski, (Random House) bestselling author of *J.D. Salinger: A Life* - www.deadcaulfields.com

"A towering literary achievement."
- Letha Hadady, author, for *The Bathsheba Deadline*

"Savor it...it may be the best, sharpest, most vivid portrait of life around the racetrack ever written."
- Ray Kerrison, *New York Post* columnist writing for the *National Star,* for *The Horsemen*

"The refugee stories Engelhard preserves are boyhood memories of an almost Tom Sawyer character... adventurous, humorous, sometimes wonderfully strange."
- Chris Leppek, *Jewish News (Denver),* for *Escape from Mount Moriah*

"What a great story. If you missed the 60s – if you missed the excitement, the passion, the radicalism, the thrills, the hopes and dreams – this book brings it all alive. I could not put it down."
- Kmgroup review, for *The Days of the Bitter End*

Dedicated to
Leslie, David, Rachel, Sarah, Toni...and Siena!

...and to the loving memory of my parents
Noah and Ida

Immeasurable gratitude to
Jeffrey Farkas

Chapter 1

Anyway, I hired her. I knew she was trouble, but I didn't know how much, for the simple reason that, unlike wall-to-wall carpet, people don't come with lifetime guarantees.

In this business, for that matter in any business, you never knew what you were getting. You hired them when they appeared reasonably lucid, communicative and reliable, though this was some task, finding anyone reliable. Some responded to the ad and never showed up and some showed up and never returned. I hired anyone still breathing. Looks didn't hurt. Sobriety helped. Most of them maybe finished high school and some had native smarts, street wisdom. You got what you paid for. We didn't pay much.

Anyhow, they all came from broken homes, these girls. These days, who didn't?

"So am I hired?" she asked.

This one was different. She was exotic, as exotic as you can get from the Price Hill section of Cincinnati, where (disgraced) Pete Rose hailed from and which was this town's bedrock of hard-working, hard-drinking, hardhat lower middle class. Price Hill was to Cincinnati what Peoria was to America. She seemed a cut above as far as intelligence, which wasn't always a plus for them or a favor to me. The smart ones never stayed very long, that was one problem, the other being that smart girls never knew when something was finished. This girl had eyes that wouldn't quit and everything about her was just plain provocative, like I'm the one getting the screen test.

Obviously, though, she was a loser, a failure, a castoff, an exile, just like the rest of us, though I'm still not sure what separates success from failure, or if there really is a difference. I have my doubts. Most times success is a cover, a performance. We're all acting except that those of us who don't know how to put it over end up here at Harry's Carpet City, upstairs in the phone soliciting department, sanctuary for the doomed. We've tried everything else.

In Cincinnati, or New York, or anywhere really, there's got to be a place for everyone, or so you'd think. I'm beginning to wonder. Some of us in this world without pity are meant to drift, which doesn't make us homeless but rootless just the same. We can't seem to catch on. We seem   destined to follow the wrong path or take the fork in the road that leads to nowhere. I blame it on luck and this means there's no one to blame.

So despite my qualms about this applicant, I had a soft spot for her – for all of them in fact.

Spooky, the way she sat there without the usual interview jitters. Maybe that was why I didn't

2

terminate (did I say "terminate?") her right on the spot, as that would have been the cowardly way out, and she would have sensed it...but so what? Hey, I was the BOSS! Except that there was something strangely intimate about a job interview, you were both revealing touches, moments and fragments of yourself and you didn't want to come off weak. Not to mention the seductive element of a job interview, like any audition. From the start you were calculating the possibilities.

With the right person, an interview was foreplay – as it was with Stephanie Eaton.

"I'd like an answer," she said.

Why was she in control? I'm the director.

She looked different from every angle. First thing you noticed was that squared-off, masculine jaw. Straight up the face was hard, lips thin, upturned nose, certainly not pretty, but all right in an across-the-river sort of way. I was willing to bet she was originally from Kentucky, Covington most likely. If she came from Newport she'd never admit it – Sin City, USA; comely Cincinnati's unruly neighbor to the south. Covington, that's where we went to get naughty and Newport? That's where we went to get very naughty. Horse country was further south, though there were some thoroughbreds in Newport, along the outskirts. They don't shoot horses in Newport. They shoot people.

She was a blonde, this one was, but a very serious, grim and gloomy blonde, even when she smiled, which was really not a grin so much as a pre-emptive showing of teeth, doing what was unnatural but required. Smiling was not her strong suit. Her teeth could use some work but so could mine. (Get me make-up!) Her eyes did the scary business. No fluttering of eyelashes, like most of them do; no blinking, in fact. Actually, they were the eyes of an animal or some beast without a soul. She was so self-assured that it could only mean that she had something on me.

I had secrets, of course.

Her name was Sonja Frick. I kept studying her application form for an acceptable reason to dismiss her. Just say no, or offer the usual excuses, like over-qualified or under-qualified, though she was neither. I didn't like her and I didn't trust her and I don't know why. The interview was going poorly, from my end at least; I was flunking. If it were me on the other seat I'd never get the part.

"I'm sure I can do whatever has to be done around here," she said scornfully, scanning the room, a room without frills that's for sure, walls that needed paint, windows that needed blinds, floors that needed linoleum that wasn't ripped. The smell? Please! She observed the desks that had been borrowed ages ago from some elementary school, still with valentine hearts and "Leroy" carved into them.

Not much else except the buzz of about a dozen girls on the phones pitching carpet.

She wasn't impressed.

"Doesn't seem too difficult," she said with a snicker. "Nothing I can't do."

I didn't mind somebody scoffing this job, so long as that somebody was me. I wasn't too thrilled when it came from someone else.

Everybody's a critic.

This wasn't brain surgery, true, but it was an honest living, even if it wasn't completely honest and wasn't much of a living.

I asked her the usual big question, hoping she'd trip up.

"Are you good with people?"

"What people?"

"People. People people."

"I don't know what you mean."

"You'd be talking to strangers all day."

"I'm good with strangers. Are they people?"

Wise guy, huh?

Her hobby, according to the application form, was reading, which certainly wasn't objectionable, except that her favorite authors were Edgar Cayce and Nostradamus, which frankly I didn't consider reading. She also liked poetry, the gloomy kind – Sylvia Plath and all the others who had committed suicide. She also mentioned Oscar Wilde and Edgar Allan Poe. Nothing cheerful here, either.

I was thinking of ways to tell her no. First of all, I didn't need the grief. Second of all, I didn't need girls with PERSONALITY. Personality was intrusive. Third, she'd never fit in. There was a group dynamics thing going on here in my boiler room and it wouldn't do to have one girl so STRANGE. The others, even the newer ones, and there were always newer ones, managed to nest in together. This one wouldn't. She felt superior, you could just tell, and she was a reflective sort. Then again, she needed the work. This was a job of last resort, even for me. Nobody – except Mona maybe – grew up with dreams of becoming a telephone solicitor, even under today's fancier term of telemarketing.

But I had already decided to say no.

"When do I start?" she said.

"How about tomorrow?"

Chapter 2

Next day she arrived as a brunette. I had hired a blonde, hadn't I? I hardly recognized her.

"I changed my hair," she said.

She stared at me for a reaction. I didn't react. What – changed hair changed person?

"I knew you didn't like it the other way."

Which was true. Though I didn't like her too much this way, either, as a brunette.

"How did you know?" I yawned.

"I'm psychic," she declared.

"That's all right," I said, turning back to the work on my desk. There was no work on my desk. I didn't want to hear any more. I'd heard it all. They all had stories and I wasn't particularly in the mood for hers, although psychic was a new wrinkle, with all kinds of dire possibilities. Most of them told you about their drunken mothers and violent fathers and runaway husbands. Amazing how nobody came from a NORMAL family. But psychic was a new one, definitely.

I didn't need a psychic. All I needed was another TELEPHONE SOLICITOR!

"Does it bother you?" she asked.

"What?"

"I see things," she said.

"I see things, too."

"I see the future."

"Sounds like fun."

"No it isn't," she said grimly.

"Whatever you say."

She said it was a curse, seeing the future; had cost her all her friends. Even her family.

"My mother threw me out of the house," she said.

I didn't want to know why.

"I predicted my father's death."

I drew a deep breath. I already knew more than I wanted to know.

You shouldn't know too much about people. Really, there's only so much room for other people's lives. Your own life is trouble enough.

She had predicted her father's death. This was not good news.

I said, "Lucky guess maybe."

"I see your future, too," she said.

This I had not bargained for.

"I don't want to know my future," I said.

"Most people do."

"I don't."

But of course now I did. What the hell was she seeing, staring at me like that?

"You're very much in love," she said.

"Most people are, off and on. You caught me on."

"She's very beautiful, but I see danger."

I gave her a sick smile. "I don't want to hear any more."

"Grave danger," she said.

"Please go to your desk."

"Don't you want to hear what's going to happen to her?"

"No I do not."

"It might help," she said, "if you knew it was coming."

"Nothing's coming. I don't believe in this stuff."

She lowered her eyes, and grew very sad.

"Do you want me to leave? I can see I'm scaring you."

On that score you didn't have to be psychic. I was scared.

"Just say the word," she said, "and I'll go home."

"Do you know her name?"

"I'll just go to my desk, all right? I've kept you long enough."

"Do you know her name?"

I should have quit while I was ahead. But I'm an actor or so I keep telling myself and we need the motivation.

"Stephanie," she said.

Another lucky guess, I figured, or she could have asked around, except that she hadn't talked to the other girls yet. Which didn't mean that there weren't a thousand other ways to find things out. There was also the chance, of course, that she had arrived at Stephanie's name through supernatural sources, from heaven or from hell. From the looks of this girl it had to be hell. My guess was that she saw grave danger for everybody...and if it was death that she saw she had to be on target, sooner or later, 100 percent of the time, and about the same percentage for all manner of illness and tragedy, since nobody went through life unscathed. But who asked? I didn't. If it was anything bad, I didn't want to hear it, especially about Stephanie.

"She's not going to die," Sonja said. "If that's what you're thinking."

"I'm not thinking."

"But it might be much worse."

Wonderful. Exactly what I needed to hear.

"Jesus Christ, lady, I don't want this!"

"Do you want me to leave?"

At this point, yes, very much. Place an ad in the paper and this is what you get. You never know. Takes all kinds all right and the longer you live the more of them you meet, from the top down to the bottom. Stephanie, of course, had been the top, or top-of-the-line as we say here in the rug business. Letting this one go, before she intruded too deeply into my life – and actually she had already done considerable damage, me wondering what tragedy was in store for Stephanie – would be the smart thing to do, but I wasn't always smart, if I was I wouldn't be here at Harry's Carpet City in Cincinnati, Ohio, I'd be on Broadway, and besides, she started to cry. I knew it was fake, a performance, but the other girls stopped dialing. Girls drew together, they bonded when one of them started to cry. Usually it was weeks or months before I had them crying. Mona – the mother of us all here at Harry's boiler room – was casting me the hard eye. Mona was like Will Rogers, only better. She never met a man, or woman, she didn't like.

I wasn't quite so generous though there was this from Philo: "Be kind, for everyone you meet is fighting a great battle."

"Only one thing I ask," I said to Sonja Frick. I was always suspicious of girls who didn't have regular names, anyway, like Mary or Sue. With a name like Sonja there had to be trouble. Yes, what's with that name, Sonja? Mystics say that a name tells everything about a person. An ox is an ox because it's an ox. I always thought a name like that, like Sonja, came from Slovakia or something, not that I ever thought about it that much. Never did, in fact, before now.

"Yes?" she whispered.

"No more of that psychic stuff."

"But I can't help it," she said. "It's a gift. Or a curse."

"Well I don't want to know what's going to happen."

"I won't tell unless you ask."

"Well I won't ask."

"People always say that," she said, smiling. She got up and walked to her desk, strangely confident.

* * *

11

Nice ass. I happened to be strictly an ass man.

But no, I thought. Not this one. With this one sex would just be the start of something or other.

* * *

Fat Jack was on the phone.

"Guess who's coming today?"

"Stop this, Fat Jack. I'm not in the mood."

"Not in the mood for Stephanie? She called me."

"Sure she did."

How many times could he play this trick? He knew what it did to me just to mention her name. Did he do it for the thrills? His thrills or mine?

"I swear it's true," he said. "She's coming, today. Just got off the phone with her."

"Knock it off."

"Will you two get it right this time?"

"Business must be slow," I said.

Chapter 3

Downstairs in the showroom Fat Jack was holding another conference with the salesmen, who were doing all the listening, Fat Jack all the talking, as was the case at least once a week, or when business was especially bad – and it always was. Business was never good. Ask any merchant. Business is always bad. Here, every day is our last. We're always going out of business.

"Another pep talk," groaned Morris Silver out of hearing range, though it always turned out that Fat Jack heard everything.

"When he was in diapers," Morris Silver said, "I was selling burial plots door-to-door in Price Hill and all around this town, making a mint off those suckers. I was selling holes in the ground, understand! Holes in the ground! Now THAT'S selling. No young pischer talks to me about being a salesman. When he was crawling on this very table I was the first member of the Million Dollar Club here. I outsold Harry Himself."

Harry Monocle was owner and founder of Harry's Carpet City and was usually referred to as Harry Himself.

Anyway, Morris Silver hadn't had a million dollar year in quite a while, like never again, for example. His best years were behind him, as opposed to, say, young Phil Coleman, one of three members of last year's Million Dollar Club, who had received a medal, from Harry Himself, for his million dollars worth of sales. He was an ACHIEVER.

Phil Coleman, sometimes known as Hot Shot, said, "Give the kid a chance. He's paid his dues."

Which was true. Back when he was still making calls, Fat Jack was the best carpet salesman in the business.

A true salesman, Harry Himself always said, is a person who sells you what you need, and what you don't need. That's a true salesman.

"Bar none," Fat Jack was saying to the assembled about his preeminence, speaking in that loud raspy voice, using his arms for emphasis and fingers for exclamation marks, much in the frantic style of Harry Monocle himself, who no longer did the day-to-day... but when he used to, boy could he give pep talks! Salesmen from competing shops used to sneak in just to get a whiff of that fire and brimstone. Everything Fat Jack knew came from Harry Himself. Harry Himself was a legend in the carpet business, now mostly retired, or rather, like God Himself, lofted to the upper heavens. In this case the fourth floor.

Harry Himself was a genius, the Einstein of sales. Even half retired, he still kept up, always suggesting new slogans and campaigns. When the Ohio River washed up miles away, he came up with a Flood Sale, though nothing here flooded, of course. He liked to say... BAD TASTE IS GOOD BUSINESS. That was his motto. Well, he had many mottos.

Actually, who could argue? He was a success, wasn't he? Who can argue with success? That's what people say.

There's no arguing with failure, either.

"That's right," Fat Jack was saying. "I could outsell you bums blindfolded, hands tied behind my aching back, and that includes you Phil, and Jake, and Roger." The Big Three. Send them out on a lead for a lousy bedroom measurement and they came back with an order for wall-to-wall, the essence of selling what wasn't needed. "Don't laugh," Fat Jack was saying. "That's why Harry Himself made me manager and not you. Because I was the best. I'm still the best. You guys – what are you? Order takers?"

Now THAT was an insult, along the lines of calling a doctor a quack, a lawyer a shyster – only this was much worse, for an order taker was nothing more than a clerk, a guy who only sold what you needed. Where was the skill or the thrill in that – or the money? Or the pride? Or the SUCCESS!

"If I'm insulting you," Fat Jack was saying, "good."

Of all the salesmen here, standing at attention, no one was more insulted than Old Lou Emmett whose reputation differed from the Big Three's in that when he had a great lead and went out for a wall-to-wall job he usually came back with a bedroom sale, and sometimes worse, like nothing.

But it wasn't always that way.

So Old Lou piped up:

"I've been in this organization thirty-five years and never has anyone called me an order taker."

Fat Jack smiled along with everybody else, seeing Old Lou getting himself so riled, stuttering and sputtering, a bad thing, since Lou had had a heart attack, and then on top of that, a stroke, so that now he was only a fraction of his old self. He could barely walk and talk, but still went out on calls out of the bigness of Fat Jack's heart. He was the company's charity case. The good thing and the bad thing about Lou was that he refused to acknowledge his diminished faculties and even denied, to himself and to the world, that he had been the victim of a heart attack, and a stroke. (Weeks apart.)

So nobody mentioned it to his face, that he was a cripple, except Fat Jack, of course. Fat Jack...Fat Jack had no couth. People shook their heads and rolled their eyes when they saw Old Lou shuffling by. (No cane for him.) Well, a few of the salesmen, like Phil Coleman, and even some customers, actually made fun of him, upon the assumption that they were immune from infirmity and old age. Some people thought those things only happened to Lou Emmett. (Just wait, Lou used to whisper to me. Everybody gets a turn.)

"I used to be big," said Lou in front of everybody. "I'm still big."

"I didn't mean you," Fat Jack said humbly, about Lou's being an order taker, and it was some doing for Fat Jack to be humble.

"You got that right," said Lou, as everybody smiled and snickered.

"We all remember you in your days of glory, Lou. We REALLY do."

Old Lou wasn't finished. "Nobody but nobody was my equal."

Nobody But Nobody was Fat Jack's TV ad campaign, as in "Nobody but Nobody Undersells Harry's Carpet City."

Fat Jack got that from Harry Himself, of course, another of Harry's mottos.

"In your day," said Fat Jack, getting less humble.

"What do you mean my day?" said Old Lou. "I'm as good today as I ever was."

"That's right, Lou. Now let me finish with these bums."

"Can I help it," said Lou, "if I get lousy leads? The bottom of the barrel? That's all I get."

All eyes turned to me. "You hear that, Eli?" Fat Jack said, eyes bright with wickedness and humor. How he loved to rub it in!

"I heard," I said.

"We need those leads from you, Eli."

"You're getting them."

"My men are STARVING, Eli," Fat Jack said in a flourish.

"They're getting leads."

"I mean verified leads."

"We're verifying them."

"Oh yeah?"

"Oh yeah."

"Well you'll have to do better, Eli. We need Hyde Park wall-to-wall, not Over the Rhine linoleum. Get some new broads up there, or something. Fresh blood. Whenever I see them, that crew you've got up there now, they're going to the bathroom. That's time, time wasted. They spend more hours in the john than upstairs in your boiler room."

He had me there, but there really was no cool way to tell girls not to go to the bathroom.

Besides, it was against the law.

Go ahead, tell a woman she can't go to the bathroom, no matter how often she goes.

Fat Jack, back to the room at large, resumed: "We all have to do better. These are tough economic times. You're all lucky to have a job, thanks to Harry Himself and his generosity. There is only one way to survive. SELL, SELL, SELL! Otherwise you die. It's not like the old days when you could just..."

Everybody always talked about the old days, as if there really were such a thing.

Chapter 4

Upstairs in the boiler room the girls were at their desks working the phones, pitching carpet to the world from a spiel I had written and which had not yet won the Nobel Prize for Literature or for Carpet. Fat Jack had made me read some book that taught POWER words. There were, for instance, no savings, only INCREDIBLE savings.

That was most of my job, updating the spiel, running the place and verifying the leads, which I hardly did anymore, I let Mona do it, most of it, because I was too bashful. I hated talking to strangers and I only had one friend. Actually I was ashamed to still be in the carpet business when some people I knew were already getting published, arguing cases before the Supreme Court, appearing on Broadway. The even more successful ones, like the bankers, industrialists and stockbrokers of my generation, were doing even better; they were already in jail!

Where was I? Running a boiler room.

Fat Jack knew the secret, that I never made calls myself, except to verify once in a while.

He said, "You're too shy? So put on an act. You're an actor." But he never insisted.

Lou was at my desk and he was sweating. The air conditioner never worked properly up here and heat rises, for sure, that was one reason, the other being that Lou liked to sweat. He always carried a big handkerchief and it was always soaked. He was also exhausted from the trek up, three flights, his daily Mount Everest.

What most people took for granted, he, now a handicapped man, had to conquer. That's how it was for him. He once confided in me the terror of walking down the wide-apart steps of a bus, and a million other things that you never thought about when you were healthy. Think about that, he liked to say. I'd rather not. Be glad you're healthy, he liked to say. Well, there is this health and there is that health. Nobody's really all that healthy.

"Sorry about that," he said, now seated next to me.

"That's okay, Lou."

"I shouldn't have put you on the spot like that, in front of everybody."

"I'll live."

"You're a pal."

"What are pals for?"

"I didn't think Fat Jack would make a federal case out of it, you know. But you know Fat Jack."

"Yeah I know Fat Jack."

"I'm not complaining about your leads. I know the girls are trying. Anything for me today?"

I turned to Mona. "Anything happening?"

20

"No," she said. "Slow, very slow. But we're getting a lot of callbacks. How you feeling, Lou?"

Lou tightened up. "What do you mean how am I feeling? I'm feeling fine. Just fine."

"Saww-ry," she said, growing red hot in the face. Nobody got flustered as easily as Mona, who was only in her late 40s, married, kids, but a virgin in every other way, as matronly a Cincinnatian as could be found, the kind of person, terrific as she was, who made you wonder – how does this person have sex? It's all so improper and unladylike. But she did have kids, so something happened.

Old Lou was angry. People were always asking him how he felt. "How are YOU feeling, Mona?"

"I'm sorry, Lou. I was just trying to be sociable."

Mona hastily got back to her dialing. Mona hated conflict, of any kind. True blue Cincinnati. Yes, there were those riots and our cops occasionally make the national headlines (not in a good way) but like Mona, Cincinnati likes to keep to itself and blushes when it gets too much attention. We don't like fame here in the Midwest. We don't have Broadway and we don't do lunch. We like beer, peanuts, baseball and patriotism.

Cleveland, actually, is another planet. It's amazing that we share the same state and the same language. Our relatives live right across the river or forgot to catch the boat from Deutschland. Plenty of us are still upstanding German/Americans and enough of us are hillbillies. You got a problem with that? We don't really care what goes on over there in Cleveland or any other place.

We're tucked nice and cuddly in the middle of this great country, this great world. We figure – you don't bother us, we don't bother you. Okay?

"What's the matter with your people?" Lou asked confidentially.

"What do you mean my people?"

"Well they're your girls."

"My girls? What do you mean my girls?"

"Never mind."

"She was only being polite."

"I don't need people feeling sorry for me."

"She only asked how you were feeling, Lou."

"Well I know what she means by that."

"She asks me that, too. She asks everybody. Everybody asks everybody. It's another way of saying hello."

"Not for me."

Lou was having a bad day. There had been many of those since the stroke.

I liked Lou, but just now I wasn't in the mood for him and frankly, as of late, I wasn't in the mood for anybody.

The phone rang and of course it was Fat Jack, Fat Jack doing Stephanie Eaton.

"Oh, Eli, I love you so much."

"Not funny," I said.

"Oh, Eli, I've thought about you every day, even out in California. The guys out there can't compare to you."

"Fat Jack, I'm hanging up."

Back to his regular voice, Fat Jack said, "Don't you wish?"

"Okay, I wish."

"She'll be here any minute, for real. Will you get it right this time or are you still a loser?"

I hung up and got back to Lou.

"I'll let you know as soon as we come up with a lead for you," I said, hoping he'd take the hint.

Lou was a sensitive guy for a salesman.

"I'd appreciate that," he said. And then he whispered, "You know, Eli, I haven't had a sale in six weeks."

"It's been that long?"

"Yes."

"But I've been giving you leads."

"The good ones? Aren't you giving them to the Big Three?"

"That's not true."

Maybe it was true, to a degree. Some leads were so good, like say out in Hyde Park, that it would be a waste to give them to Old Lou, who simply didn't have it anymore, so you gave him the marginal ones just to keep him busy. Just to keep him thinking he was still alive and ticking. Fat Jack considered him already dead. Fat Jack was a very subtle guy and when he saw Lou coming, shuffling along as he did, he'd say, "Here comes our cripple." Or, "Dead salesman walking." As I said, Fat Jack was a very subtle person and he'd be on my back if he caught me wasting good leads on Old Lou, though once in a while

I sneaked one through, and sure enough, nine times out of ten, Lou would return with excuses.

(Lou? I always figured that he'd been delivered to me by Arthur Miller.)

I had suggested to Fat Jack that we send a CLOSER to accompany Lou on his appointed rounds, somebody to finish off a sale – there were people like the Big Three who specialized in that, it was an extraordinary skill – and Fat Jack said, "YOU propose it to him," meaning that Lou would have a fit at the insinuation that he wasn't salesman enough to close deals on his own anymore.

"Far be it from me to make accusations," Lou said. "It just seems when they go out on a call for you, ends up in a sale."

"It's all luck, Lou."

"Me – sometimes the people aren't even home. Like that time in Amberly Village, and you call that verifying?"

"She was a new girl, who got us that lead. I fired her."

Do I tell him the truth? Do you tell a man the truth, that he's kaput? Not me. I won't give that line and I won't take that part or play that scene. As for that new girl, the real reason I had fired her was because after we had made love that one time she thought it was time to get married and even went around telling the others that we were engaged. Her name was Sue. Or maybe it was Mary.

"Just get me some good leads, will you pal?" He slapped me on the back. "We're pals, right?"

24

"We're pals, Lou."

Slapping me on the back had taken up much of Lou's energy and he started coughing again, which drove me nuts; I was afraid he'd never stop or start choking and that would be the end of him. He really was sad to behold. You kept blessing God that you weren't in his condition. But it worried you what happened to people. Lou was a warning of things to come. It's great that we get to live longer – but for what reason?

Lou walked over to Mona and kissed her on the cheek. She got red in the face and kissed him back. "Friends?" he said.

"We'll always be friends, Lou," Mona said. "You and I go back too far for it to be otherwise."

"You're my girl. Eli, you're my pal, right?"

"We're pals, Lou."

Chapter 5

Downstairs I said to Fat Jack, "Are you out of your mind?"

"Just ask her," he said, breathing into my face, an old habit of his when he wanted to trouble me, and he always did. We were in the Oriental Department, Oriental rugs, that is, which was deserted, since nobody bought Oriental rugs when the economy was bad, and even when the economy was good, which it never was. Oriental drew a very specific clientele, classy types, like Stephanie, oh well.

"A favor," Fat Jack said. "All I ask is a favor. I do plenty for you. The fact that I keep you employed is a favor. All you use those girls for is to fuck 'em." He had me in a schoolyard bear hug, letting go only after I tapped him silly in the balls. He said, "That's money out of my pocket, those girls I hire for you. I pay for your pussy."

Fat Jack thought I ran a regular harem up there. Everybody thought so, in fact.

"I'm not playing pimp for you, Fat Jack. You want her. You ask her."

He wanted Marie, that sleek little blonde from Newport, Kentucky I had brought on about two months ago. (The turnaround in telephone soliciting, excuse me, telemarketing, was something terrific.) Fat Jack was an outrageous guy, and proud of it, witness those TV commercials in which he bragged that he must be CRAZY, CRAZY, CRAZY for slashing prices like that, even pulling his hair and grimacing all over the place just to show how crazy he was, but I wasn't prepared for this. He wanted to rent one of my girls. He was a married man. A pillar, a very wide pillar, of the community.

"So I'll do just that," he said. "I'll ask her myself."

"She won't go for it," I said. "She knows you're married."

"She's from Kentucky, isn't she?"

"Yeah."

"She'll do it," he said, punching me in the ribs.

"Because she's from Kentucky?"

"Because I'm offering her a hundred bucks."

"She's no whore."

"They're all whores."

"Girls from Kentucky?"

"Girls from everywhere!"

"Ten bucks says she turns you down."

"Make it a hundred," he said. "Make it a THOUSAND."

"The kind of money you pay me?"

"All right. Ten. Eli, you may be the biggest Romeo in Cincinnati, but you're naïve as hell. You're a baby."

Frankly, I considered that a compliment.

* * *

The rumor was that Marie was in love with me, which was a no-no. Take them to bed if you must, but no tie-ups, or like the guy before me said – and he didn't even believe in taking them to bed – "Don't piss in the pot you drink from." Well, I did much pissing into that pot, not that I was proud of it, but what were you going to do? Marie and I had made love only once, most of the seducing coming from her, as when she said, "Can I go home with you?" She was a sweet kid, quiet, well built, actually very well built, terrific breasts, and I happened to be strictly a breast man.

I had been putting her off for weeks because I didn't want to hurt her, Marie. I'd be using her.

"No," I said bravely. But she followed me to the car. How long can you go on being a hero?

She did all the work in bed and was trying very hard to please and in a strange, detached way it was quite wonderful, pure sex that it was, and to think how completely she had given herself and was offering herself, like a sacrifice; there was nothing she'd refuse me. Which made it all quite sad. I wasn't using sex for passion anymore, or even for pleasure, certainly not for love. Just to kill time.

Until Stephanie came back. She always did, did come back, although there is always a first time, or do I mean a last time?

It was all about Stephanie. Nothing else counted, nothing and nobody. Only Maishe would understand.

Maybe not. Maishe was still Joe College, living the frat life, even though he had already matriculated and was still matriculating from one girl to the next so maybe he'd fail to understand this obsession of mine over a single woman – but what a woman! Maishe still tallied his conquests. Maishe still kept score.

I kept telling him it's getting late. Soon there'll be no one left to laugh at our pranks and buy our charms. This too shall pass.

* * *

The girls were making plans for lunch. That's a routine that has them going back and forth. Mona seldom went with them so there was no one to make a decision. They decided, finally, on Frank's Diner on Vine Street and asked Sonja the Psychic to join them. She declined, the third straight day she had done so, and instead, after the room emptied out, sat there at her desk occasionally reading a book and occasionally staring at me.

She was reading the short stories of F. Scott Fitzgerald. How come?

"Because I knew you liked him."

"How did you know?"

"I told you. I'm psychic."

I shouldn't have asked. But oh my gawd! She is. She is psychic, or something.

"Why don't you go out for lunch?"

"What about you?"

"I don't eat lunch."

"That's good enough for me," she said.

I asked her if she was getting along with the other girls.

"I'd rather read," she said. "I find that more stimulating."

"Except that real people are what books are all about."

"I'm waiting to meet Stephanie," she said smiling.

"Why?"

"Just because."

"Just because why?"

"Are you afraid I'm going to hurt her?"

No I wasn't. Not until she brought it up.

"Hurt her?"

"Well I know you think I'm some kind of weirdo. Everybody else does."

"Why would you say anything about hurting Stephanie?"

"Forget it," she said.

Do I fire her now? Practically very day I was on the verge of making that move. Except that so far she had given me no solid reason. She wasn't that bad on the phones. She was okay. She got us a couple of leads a day and that's about all that can be expected, and some of the girls were lucky to get that many in a week. She gave good phone, as Fat Jack would say.

"I want to know why people think you're weird."

"Because people think I'm...oh never mind!"

"Please. Go on."

"All right. Some people think I'm dangerous."

"Well are you?"

"Sometimes. Sometimes trouble seems to follow me."

"Like when?"

"I told you I predicted my father's death. My mother thinks I made him die." She laughed at that, though I wasn't sure at what in particular, her father's death or her mother's suspicions. "Same thing with a boyfriend I once had. They always blame me. All I do is tell people what I see. But they always blame me. You'll see. You'll blame me for Stephanie, too."

Oh Please!

Fat Jack called from downstairs, from down in the store, the showroom as it was called, first to ask if I was giving good leads to Lou. "Don't waste them on that cripple," he said. I defended Lou but it was no use. Lou was a cripple and Fat Jack was a crude son of a bitch and there was nothing you could do about either. The second reason was this: He wanted me to send down Marie so that he could proposition her.

"Get her down yourself, Fat Jack."

"Put her on the phone."

"To hell with you," I said, and hung up.

A minute later he was upstairs.

Mona said, "Well lookie who's here."

"Quit yapping and get us leads," Fat Jack howled. "Stay on those phones. LEADS, LEADS, LEADS. We're STARVING."

"Oh you," said Mona. "You don't scare me."

Mona was used to Fat Jack's entrances and Fat Jack's shenanigans. He's all talk, she liked to say.

"Well I better scare you because I OWN you."

"Oh shush."

"You, you, you, you, you, you, you, you, you," Fat Jack said, pointing to each girl individually. "I own all of you."

The girls were giggling, those familiar with Fat Jack's outbursts and hip to his whimsy. Except for Sonja Frick.

"What's with her?" Fat Jack asked me, privately, as soon as order was restored.

"Who?"

"That new broad."

"She's psychic."

"She gives me the creeps."

"Me, too."

"So why did you hire her?"

"People haven't been breaking the doors down to work here, Fat Jack."

"I didn't know we were that desperate. I'd keep away from her, Eli."

"I intend to."

"That's fatherly advice. That girl's trouble. I can smell it a mile off. Dump her."

"Not just yet. She's got us a few leads."

"Give her a couple of days and send her home. Spooky. You hear me?"

"I hear you."

"That's one conquest you don't need."

Speaking of conquests, Fat Jack strolled over to Marie, whispered something, and they marched out together.

"What's that all about?" Mona whispered, baffled and flustered.

"Nothing," I said.

"She's trying," said Mona. "She really is."

"She's not being fired, Mona. That's not what this is about."

"Oh? What is it about?"

"Never mind."

Mona was the mother of us all, up here in the boiler room. If Mona had an inkling of what's going on in the world, she didn't let on. She was no Born Again Christian. No reason to be born again when the first time took. She attended church regularly. She worked without complaining, ever, about anything. She was not dumb, not at all, she had neighborhood wisdom and if there were troubles beyond her scope, made no difference as long as she was home in time to make dinner.

Marie came back and asked if she could talk to me outside in the hallway. Okay. There, in the hallway, she said, "Mind if I take the afternoon off?"

"You're not feeling well?"

"Something like that."

Who could blame her? If I were a girl and Fat Jack propositioned me, I'd be sick, too.

After she left I phoned Fat Jack to tell him that he owed me ten bucks. But he wasn't in, either.

Chapter 6

"You owe me ten bucks," he said, grabbing me around the neck and twisting us both to the ground in the Linoleum Department, never mind the customers who came for carpet when instead a fight broke out. "Forget the money. I'll take this in payment." He grabbed a pair of scissors from the counter and cut my tie in half. Back home I had an entire collection of half-ties, mementos.

"I don't believe you," I said.

"Ask her. It's a done deal."

I really didn't believe him. Marie was no innocent, but she did have working class values, didn't she? A hundred bucks and she was his?

It really shouldn't be that easy, and maybe that's another reason why I was so nuts about Stephanie.

For her, yes, you would have to write a symphony, maybe Beethoven's Ninth. (I'm not sure, though, if it worked for him personally, Beethoven, possibly celibate to his grave.)

"The deal is this," Fat Jack said about his arrangement with Marie.

"Do I have to hear?"

He grabbed me by the collar. I grabbed him right back.

"Yes you have to hear," he said. "You have to grow up."

"I'm listening."

"It's already started, and she was great. Eli, the greatest piece of ass I ever had." What terms we used to ascribe the beautiful art of lovemaking – piece of ass. What happened to courtliness, chivalry and romance? When did we get so crude? But who was I to talk? I had my own reputation.

"You're a jerk, you know," Fat Jack continued, shaking me by the lapels and me shaking him right back. "She spent half the time crying, about how much she was in love with you. She said she was doing it for the hundred bucks because she thought that's what YOU wanted."

This made me sick. "She was doing it for me?"

"Forget that."

"Forget that? Did you give her that impression, that I was in on this?"

"I never said a word about you."

"Did you straighten her out?"

"It didn't matter."

"Well it matters to me that she thinks..."

"She'll do anything for you, Eli."

"Did she take the hundred bucks?"

"What do you think?"

"I don't know. You tell me."

"Of course she did. Eli, girls were made for fucking. Who knows that better than you, cockhound of the Midwest."

"Come on."

"That's all they're good for."

"Your mother, your wife, your sister, your daughter..."

"That's different. We're not talking family, you yutz. We're talking girls."

"Oh them!"

"You're judging me? You whose conquests number in the hundreds? The THOUSANDS?"

"None of my doing."

"Oh – it's that you're so irresistible they can't keep their hands off you?"

"No, it's a winning streak. You should have been around when I had the acne."

"So now it's catch-up time?"

"No, Fat Jack. It's just a hot streak, like the Reds when they've got it going."

Fat Jack wouldn't understand about the Cincinnati Reds since he was the only local who cared nothing for baseball. For the rest of us the Reds were the beginning and the end. Our lives were tied to the Reds. Fat Jack once got a couple of free tickets and gave them to me and I took Stephanie to the game. Stephanie loved baseball though she wasn't sure what team they were playing against or even what league they were in. She asked, during the game, if the Reds were as big as the Yankees and I said, who are the Yankees? Which set her straight, I think.

When one of our guys hit a home run everyone got up and cheered and she just sat there, not out of disrespect; she just didn't know.

She was more used to debutante balls and tennis and lunch on the veranda at the country club.

So I explained that you're supposed to stand and cheer when someone hits a homerun, which she did, when someone from the other team did. Oh well, my mistake.

"Well I'm playing catch-up to you, Eli," Fat Jack said. "You don't have to pay for it; I do. So what? Nature was kind to you. Me, I'm ugly. So I pay. Does that make your conquests purer, more righteous than mine? I don't think so. You use your looks for barter, I use money. We're both trading on what we've got to offer. So don't be getting superior on me, Eli."

"But wasn't it rotten to make her think she was doing ME a favor by screwing YOU?"

"I didn't make her think anything, Eli. She drew her own conclusions."

He said I could still have her.

"Except on Mondays."

He punched me in the arm. I punched him in the belly.

"You think I care?" I said.

"I know you don't. That's the trouble with you, Eli. Ever since you came back from New York."

"What about before?"

"Before you weren't so terrific, either."

"Thanks, Fat Jack."

"But at least you had Stephanie. That's why you came back, right? For Stephanie."

"Maybe."

"Also because you couldn't make it there as an actor." He started pushing me around with his belly, his favorite sport. Fat Jack had some belly, hence his nickname. "You left a loser and you came back a loser. Not that I'm calling you a loser. Between then and now, you also lost Stephanie."

"Thanks for reminding me, Fat Jack."

"Of what?"

"That I'm a loser."

He punched me in the shoulder and kept at it until I gave him one to the belly. He grabbed and twisted my tie.

"You've given up," he said, "and I know why. You're trying to punish yourself for that other thing."

THAT OTHER THING was the possible killing of a man. I don't know for sure. It was a blur. The man was on 72nd Street in New York, between Second and Third Avenues, it was one a.m., I was returning from my night shift as a waiter in Greenwich Village, between auditions, and saw the man beating a boy of about eight years old. He told me it was his son so it was all right.

I said, "You're killing the boy."

He said, "Pardon me?"

"You're killing the boy."

"Pardon me?"

"I can't let you do this."

"Pardon me?"

I blocked his fist from landing another blow to the kid's head. He took a swing at me with his free arm. I hit him in the throat. He grabbed his throat, gagged, staggered, went down, and was out. That sudden, that fast. The cops came. I was arrested but let go, and never knew why.

I never found out what happened to the kid. I only knew that I had hurt a man unconscious and did not know (to this day) if he ever came around. I had good cause to do what I did. I never could watch this stuff, even in movies or on TV, I mean the abuse of children, or women, and here it was in real life. But when you hurt someone like that (did I take a life?) you do something cosmic. You rearrange the stars. You also rearrange the universe that is you. You can never be the same again. But they let me go, the cops did, and charged me with nothing. Very strange. They never even gave me a chance to explain the correctness of my action.

The cops came after I phoned it in. They checked out the guy, and called for an ambulance, but someone said it may be too late. Anyway, that bruiser, they took him off, hospital or morgue. They took the kid to the hospital, that much I did know about the kid. They took me to a precinct station, locked me in a detention cell and three hours later said I was free to go. I wouldn't need a lawyer. I wouldn't need a thing. Goodbye. I was free. As if nothing had happened.

Maybe the kid had told them everything, how I had stepped in for him.

Maybe the guy had a long rap sheet, or mob connections, and they wanted him dead, or locked up. Whatever.

Maybe he was a crooked cop and they wanted all of it hushed. (That still makes the most sense to me.)

Maybe a thousand other reasons.

The point was, I wasn't guilty.

But I wasn't innocent, either.

Only Fat Jack knew about this. Only Fat Jack because I trusted him. In business he'd skin you alive. But man to man he was fiercely honest and trustworthy. "You figured the courts didn't punish you, God didn't punish you, so you're punishing yourself," he was now saying. "I can imagine what it's like living with that memory. You must have nightmares by the hours."

Which I couldn't deny.

"But you can't live your whole life in retreat," he said, "in a funk, over something you once did. We all once did something."

Chapter 7

"It's not good," said Mona after all the others had gone home.

Mona was in a very serious mood and she worried me when she got that way. I was tired. I had a headache. It was hot. The leads still weren't coming. The salesmen were complaining. Even the Big Three, Phil Coleman among them, were going slow from regular walk-in business downstairs. Fewer people were responding to the newspaper and TV ads. When the economy was bad luxuries like carpet were the first things people stinted on. Everybody complained how bad business was. The stock market was down to record lows. The temperature was up to record highs. Every year people said the stock market had never been so low and the temperature had never been so high. I hadn't been around when the world was perfect, but it must have been perfect since people kept saying things had never been so bad before.

I didn't care. I had spent the day thinking about Stephanie. That'll get you very high and very low.

"I know what you're going to say," I said to Mona.

"Then get rid of her."

We weren't talking about Marie. We were talking about Sonja the Psychic. When Mona took a dislike to someone, it was time for alarm.

I told Mona that I felt sorry for Sonja.

"She's broke. She's working hard. I can't fire her."

Mona said she was a bad influence on the girls, scaring them with her spooky talk, but mostly with her big-eyed glances and silences that were getting creepier by the day. She told one of the girls, Tina, that she, Tina, had only a short time to live, and this affected Tina very badly.

"I can imagine," I said.

"And there's lots you can't imagine."

"Oh?"

"She's falling for you, you know, as they all do eventually."

"I never take that too seriously."

"This time you should, Eli. That one spooks me."

"Fat Jack said the same thing."

"Well for once he's right."

"But she hasn't done anything."

"Do we have to wait until she does?"

"What's that supposed to mean?"

"She's been confiding in me, and some of the other girls, saying you two are DESTINED."

"Me and Sonja?"

"You have no idea how much she hates Stephanie."

"She's never met Stephanie."

"Yes she has. She SEES things, remember? She sees you two married, living happily ever after – after she gets Stephanie out of the way. She says sooner or later you're going to realize that Stephanie is really ugly, and if you don't realize that yourself, she'll do something to prove the point."

"Like what?"

"I don't know, Eli, but I'd take it as a threat."

"That's crazy, Mona."

"Exactly, Eli. This one's crazy."

"Come on, Mona," I laughed. "You think she's a witch or something?"

"Yes."

* * *

Fat Jack called to ask if I was busy, which was a laugh, I was never busy, but as a question it was usually a prelude to a rotten task. In fact he always asked if I was busy and I always said yes and he always laughed. We had this joke going about how wrong I was for this job and how wrong I was for practically everything. But he put up with me because – hell, I don't know.

"Yes I'm busy," I said.

He wondered if I could take a few minutes of my precious time to walk across the street, to Ben's Smoke and News Shop, and bring back those Cuban cigars Harry Himself had specially ordered. I thought about that for a while. Am I an errand-boy? No, I don't do errands. I am an artist, nearly made the second cut off-Broadway and my photo is still floating around. That phone call may still come any day. I am an actor!

Forget that, if we must, but wasn't I supposed to be some sort of an EXECUTIVE around here? I wore a suit! All right I didn't, but I could if I wanted to. I was supposed to. Even if I wasn't an EXECUTIVE I was in charge of an office, a department – I had a STAFF. I had a BUDGET, even though I never knew what it was. Yes, I was head of a DEPARTMENT. I was a department HEAD.

"Well?"

"I'm really too busy."

"Eli, it'll only take a few minutes. Please. For me. Do it for me."

"So why don't you go?"

"I got customers down here. Please Eli, this time I'm serious."

Also, and this was strange, he had to run over and drop something off at his synagogue. We did not talk religion here at Harry's Carpet City, or practically anywhere else in Cincinnati. Not that it was taboo. It was impolite. We were family and religion causes friction around the table. We had Saturday people, Sunday people, and even Friday people, but it was pretty much don't ask don't tell. Beginning with the Our Crowd dynasties of Ochs (newspapers) and Lazarus (department stores), of which Emma was a member, the Jews of Cincinnati were Episcopalian.

"I really am serious," said Fat Jack. "Harry needs those cigars."

Yes he was, and I couldn't remember the last time Fat Jack had been so serious.

"Why can't somebody else go?"

"Everybody's tied up. Come on, Eli."

"Is this a test?"

If it was, it wouldn't be coming from Fat Jack, who'd never fire me, on his own. We had an understanding, that we were brothers, not technically, but brothers, with all the (mostly good-natured) bickering; living out our lives in someone else's world. Fat Jack played the conventional middle class game, but he knew the absurdity of it all.

I had quit once, a few summers back, against Fat Jack's advice and it took only a few weeks to get me completely broke, so broke that I finally went tottering to the unemployment office and waited in those lines with other people who were broke just like me, the losers in this war of economics, and here you are in that universe where you're just a number and always waiting in the wrong line.

You are being processed, branded just like sheep, with the same sensitivity.

Soon, after about three hours, I had to go to the bathroom. I asked the guy in front of me, wearing a Pittsburgh Pirates t-shirt, if he'd save my place till I got back and he nodded okay. In the bathroom I threw up and when I got back my place in line was taken. Pittsburgh, figured.

I inched closer and now there was just one person ahead of me, then it was my turn, and just at that moment I fell back and passed out. When I recovered nobody helped me get up because you'd lose your place in line. So never mind the unemployment – I probably didn't qualify anyway – but now the job was to get home. Drive? No, not in this condition, woozy as I was. Whom to call? I tried Maishe. He wasn't home at either place, where he regularly lived or on campus. Next I tried Fat Jack. He was there in 15 minutes and wasted no time telling me I told you so, you yutz!

"You're not cut out for this life," was what he said.

But he was there; he showed up.

"No test," he now said. "We're only talking cigars, Eli. CIGARS!"

"You know it's not cigars we're talking about."

"You could have been there and back by now."

"Like any running dog."

Fat Jack sighed. "Forget it – I'll go myself."

"Never mind. So happens I was just on my way over to Ben's anyway for some pipe tobacco."

Fat Jack: "We needed all this grief?"

Chapter 8

Ben was behind the counter smoking a cigar.

He used to say: "People tell me if I smoke I'll die. So if I don't smoke I'll live?"

Ben was in his late 70s. He did more than run a smoke and news shop. Ben (self-educated) was well-read, an intellectual, a philosopher, an iconoclast. He worshipped Mencken, Voltaire and Erasmus. He could quote them all and from Erasmus he learned that cynicism was the highest form of truth. Only one president, in his view, was worthy of the office, John F. Kennedy. The rest were bums.

When I walked in he winked at me. He was telling a customer I'd never seen before (only regulars frequented the place): "Sure everybody used to come in here, back in the old days. Duke Snider came in here once. Joe Louis was here. Rocky Marciano. Duke Snider. Everybody."

"You already said Duke Snider," said the guy, who didn't know the protocol.

"That's right. Duke Snider. Big Klu. Wally Post. Johnny Temple. They were all here. Those were ballplayers."

"Well I seen Joe DiMaggio and Mickey Mantle," said the guy, who was obviously from New York and passing through, probably thinking he was in the HEARTLAND. Probably thinking he was in Cleveland. They all thought Cleveland was Cincinnati. They thought Ohio was Kansas. I remembered that from New York. People would say, "You're the guy from...Cleveland, right?"

Hank, Ben's partner, came over to help out, saying, "Had some of the finest jockeys here, too."

"Best jockeys are in New York. I seen Eddie Arcaro."

That made Ben laugh. "Mister, Eddie Arcaro is from Cincinnati. Cincinnati's his hometown."

"Anyway, that was a long time ago..."

"That's correct, Mister. Everything was a long time ago. You seen a boxer like Joe Louis? You seen a ballplayer like Big Klu? You seen jockeys like Arcaro, Longden, Shoemaker? Don't give me Vasquez. I'm talking jockeys. You want to talk writers? Gimme a Hemingway! Gimme a Lardner. You wanna talk presidents? Gimme a Roosevelt. You wanna talk horses? Gimme a Kelso, a Dr. Fager. You young people, you came too late. Everything's ALREADY HAPPENED."

Ben gave me another wink. For some reason, even though he could be my grandfather, Ben considered me part of his generation, at least he bestowed upon me the honor of his generation's wisdom, seeing in me, perhaps, something of a tattered individual. Also, I smoked, the last to do so of MY generation.

"Tell me Roosevelt once came into your shop," said the New Yorker.

"As a matter of fact he did. Everybody who was anybody was here at least once."

When the guy left Ben said, "In the old days...you know how they sent in the results from River Downs? By carrier pigeon."

"Those were the days all right," I said, whatever they were, those days.

"You came for Harry's cigars?"

"Yup."

"He's too good to come for them himself?"

"Yup."

"Harry's all right. I remember when he first started out, from the back seat of a Chevy selling remnants. He's all right. Not like some of those salesmen of his."

"They're all right."

"They're wise guys. They respect nothing. Do any of them read?"

"Contracts for wall-to-wall."

Ben liked that. "You're all right, Eli. Someday..."

"Yeah."

"You're not like the other salesmen."

"I'm not a salesman."

"I know. You're an actor. Matter of fact, you look like William Holden, doesn't he Hank?"

Ben said that to me at least once a week. Also, "One day, Eli, your name will be up in lights."

"Or up on the post office's most wanted bulletin board," said Hank.

Ben handed over Harry's box of cigars – Cuban and contraband, but Ben had contacts. He could go to jail if word got out.

"What can they do to me at my age," Ben said.

Hank already had some history with the authorities.

"They've done enough," said Hank.

The shop was raided now and then even though Ben and Hank counted cops and politicians among their clientele.

Chapter 9

I called it boiler room fever, this thing that happened when people were thrown in together eight hours a day, five days a week and turned familiarity into lust. Most affairs, and plenty of marriages, had nothing to do with storybook love, as much as the fact that you were here and she was here. Maybe I had a bit of an ego, but I wasn't stupid enough to think that my looks and my charms lured all these women to me. My greatest asset was that I was here and another guy wasn't.

So it was no terrific compliment when they'd get that washy look in the eyes and find excuses to hang around your desk and come in early and stay late and suddenly wear tight sweaters and short skirts. They'd show leg, flash smiles, stare dreamily into your eyes, just as Sonja started doing more and more.

"Are you sure you want me to call Avondale?" Sonja asked. "I mean it's mostly black."

The girls worked from a Criss-Cross Directory off a new-fangled computer database, which differed from a regular phone book in that it provided complete addresses, too, and by neighborhood, which was valuable information in the world of telephone soliciting as it more or less told you who was rich and who was poor, who was carpet and who was linoleum, who was area rug and who was wall-to-wall.

"I mean it's such a waste of time and I'm getting tired of all these rejections."

Which I could sympathize with since rejection was the name of this game. Fifty percent of the people said no even before the girls had a chance to start their pitch and 49 percent simply hung up. Not much slack. That's the carpet business, at least from the phone soliciting end, and that's show business. Heck, it's all the same. New York and Cincinnati are not that far apart.

It was the end of the day and the others had already left except for Mona who had seen this coming.

She was trying to outstay Sonja.

"We'll talk about it tomorrow," I said to Sonja.

But Sonja didn't move. Only her skirt did, upwards.

"Well," said Mona, "guess I'd better be moving along and make dinner. Got three starving sons."

Her fourth son, of course, was in the Marines. Mona came in each day with the same smile and the same dress, one of those dresses full of flowers – but always freshly washed and pressed. Her husband was on Railroad disability. He'd choked on some food while on the job, had to be rushed to the hospital where they had to cut open his throat. Even then she came in smiling and cheerful and now it was odd how she talked about having four sons, when in fact she only had two still at home. What she meant (unintentionally) was her husband.

"But before I go," she said, "can I have a word with you Eli?"

Out in the hallway she said, "I know what's going on."

"So do I, Mona. Don't worry."

"Don't let her get started on you. She's like syrup."

Back at my desk I asked Sonja what I could do for her, it was time to close up shop. She asked if I had seen the latest Woody Allen movie. I said I thought Woody Allen was vastly overrated and that that was the trouble with this country, people were either vastly overrated or vastly underrated.

"I guess you consider yourself among the latter," she said.

"I didn't mean it that way. It was a general observation."

"But you are underrated. I know you have talent. They tell me you're really an actor."

"Yeah, like everybody else."

"You really don't belong here, do you?"

"Yes I do. Where we are is where we belong."

"You know what I mean."

I sighed an actor's sigh and said, "Well, time to go home."

"Have you ever read Oscar Wilde?"

"I guess."

"What about *The Picture of Dorian Gray*?"

"What about it?" I asked.

"You know, how people aren't the same inside as they appear on the outside? Outside he was beautiful. Inside he was a monster. Like that picture showed him to be. Remember?"

"I suppose."

"Doesn't that fascinate you?" she said.

"Not really."

"I mean how people, even beautiful people, really are inside. Some people need a picture to show them the truth."

"What are you getting at here, Sonja?"

"Nothing. Except that some people you know may not be as beautiful as you think. Maybe you need a picture."

"Can you be more specific?"

"Not right now."

I faked a yawn. "Time to go home."

She sprung it like a loaded pistol. "Can I go home with you?"

I said no.

"Why not?"

I explained that I lived in Mount Adams, which might not be her style. My apartment was a dump.

"I don't care. I want to see how you live."

"Some other time."

"You're afraid of me."

"No I'm not."

"Mona. She's talking against me. I know what she's been saying to you."

"Really, I have to go."

"I'm going with you."

I shrugged. I've got to stop shrugging.

* * *

She said my place wasn't so bad, like I needed this review. She checked out the kitchen and the kitchen table that I never used; so much easier to eat over the counter. She eyed the box spring and mattress in the living room, which served as my bed and my bed-room. This wouldn't get that far, that was a promise. I owed it to myself to pass up at least one triumph.

She boiled us tea. She said: "I guess I'm just one of those girls trying to get your mind off Stephanie. Seems nobody can replace her in your heart, but boy how they try!"

"Don't know what you're talking about," I said lazily.

"You know, of course, that all the girls are crazy for you."

"It's a living," I said, quoting Clark Gable.

"Was Stephanie that good in bed?"

"I never took her to bed."

That sent her laughing, a strange, deep, husky, masculine, unholy laugh.

"You mean all a girl has to do is NOT go to bed with you?"

"Maybe so."

"Wait till I pass that word around."

"I wish you would."

"Well I think the only way you can really get to know another person is to go to bed with them."

"I don't think so."

"That's the only way to get to know me."

"Come on, Sonja. I'm taking you home."

"No you're not."

"Yes I am."

"Naked?"

Off came her sweater, skirt, bra, panties and indeed she was naked. Another naked woman. She slipped under the covers as if she belonged there and that I resented most of all, the proprietorship of her actions. I lit up a cigarette. Then I got up and walked out, out of the house. If she wanted my bed she could have it but without me in it, but she was right behind me, still naked but now screaming to the high heavens, here in the open street, hysterical.

Now Cincinnati is a most conservative town, meaning relatively upright and uptight, the Queen City in many respects, utterly GERMAN it its adherence to propriety – but this is Mount Adams where I live, a section of town the rest of the dowdy population tolerates as the accepted (Bohemian) delinquent in the family. Mount Adams was our Greenwich Village, except for the yuppies who had begun taking over.

So this woman running naked and screaming down the street drew only this rebuke: "Keep it down, please."

Even, "Fuck you, please."

I finally wrestled her back in and got her dressed. She grew calm. Maybe too calm.

Even when she was hysterical she was in control.

"You're too good for me? Is that it?" she said.

"I'm just not in the mood."

"You'd be in the mood with Stephanie, wouldn't you?"

"Please keep Stephanie out of this."

"I'm afraid that's too late."

"I wish you wouldn't bring up her name. She's nothing to you."

"She's everything to me, and yes, I know how you hate it when I use her name. I defile her name, don't I?"

Entirely correct.

"Well listen to this. Stephanie, Stephanie, Stephanie, Stephanie, Stephanie..."

I felt like punching her in the mouth.

"I'm taking you home."

"Coward."

When I dropped her off, she said, "We're not finished, you and me."

"Good night."

"Sweet dreams," she said.

"Thanks."

"Keep dreaming of Stephanie. While you can."

When I got back home I sprayed Lysol all over my bed but some odors just don't go away.

* * *

She said she didn't know what got into her.

"I'm so sorry," she said.

We were in the hallway outside the boiler room and she was crying and it seemed sincere; it sure was vehement, tears and everything; more than ready for her close-up. "Please forgive me," she kept saying. "Please. I didn't mean a word I said. I don't know what got into me. Please don't fire me. Please. I have no money. I really, really, really need this job."

I had already made up my mind to fire her, but that wouldn't necessarily be the same as getting rid of her, which was what I was really, really, really after. Getting people out of your life wasn't as simple as getting them in. All I asked from most people was hello and goodbye. Who needed that stuff in between?

"Just let me get back to my desk. I'll be a good girl. I'll never bother you again. One more chance."

I nodded.

I've got to stop nodding.

* * *

Denise, one of my best girls, and spunky as a pup, said: "Eli, are you aware that you talk to yourself?"

Mona laughed.

"You do," said Denise. "Don't he?"

"Yes you do," said Mona in between making her calls.

I had been sitting at my desk half asleep. I had just finished reading the paper, *The Cincinnati Enquirer*, which always depressed me, not the *Enquirer*, but finishing it, as reading the paper was something to do, something to hide in, and once it was done, once you were finished reading about other people's troubles, you had to face your own.

I said, "I do not talk to myself."

"Yes you do," said Denise in the kind of mock agitation familiar down home. "You pace and you talk to yourself."

"What do I say?"

"You say, nobody cares."

"No that's not what I say. I say, I don't care."

"No. That's not what you say. Ain't that right, Mona?"

"Keep me out of this."

All that may be true after all, about how I talk to myself and keep saying nobody cares. Faith, in people, in God, is a skill I've never mastered. I know how to curse but don't know how to pray. From birth to death, it's all random. If there is a plan, I wish someone would hurry up and tell me what it is. This sure can't be it. Why even our doctors of divinity tell us that we're cursed from birth, so what salvation can we count on except a decent paycheck?

Denise had just gotten married to a guy who did phone soliciting for a company that sold recliners on Vine Street, a sleazy operation known as Seats Galore. The guy who ran the place, Stone Kiley, was a shady character who also pitched siding and other useless furnishings from the same boiler room. Mona's mother-in-law worked for him. Before her marriage, Denise and I carried on for a good three months, before I found out that she was jail bait. She made me swear to keep the secret, and of course I would, since she had an even bigger secret on me – more than once I had transported her home, across state lines, into Newport, Kentucky, and how many years was that worth!

The sad thing was that Denise had an overturned something or other in her vagina, so she could never have regular intercourse. But I was happy that she had found herself a husband and that they were working something out to get themselves some children. There was so much to learn about women. They were so much more complicated than the rest of us. They all had their own stories, so many of them sad. In fact I never met a woman with a happy story to tell. Once you got to know them.

Everybody's got a story.

Chapter 10

Old Lou was coming up the stairs, slowly, each step another obstacle.

"How is everybody?"

"Fine, Lou," said Mona.

He smiled at the crew. Not a single one of the girls smiled back. They never did.

I once gave them a lecture on that, about being kind. Lou never chose old age and illness. You could be next.

"What the hell happened to manners?" I said. "Everybody's so damned surly all of a sudden!"

Which seemed to be especially true of the young, and the old. Frankly, I could understand old people getting mean-spirited, they had lived a life and had had to do battle, but it didn't make sense seeing young people getting so hard-nosed. Even some of the girls who came in here barely out of high school showed signs of bitterness and it made you wonder if they were reacting from abuses of the past or – or whether they were wisely and genetically anticipating the road ahead. Anyway, that helped for a while, that sermon I gave about Lou, and Lou started getting good receptions, but to keep it going I'd have to be Jesus Christ once every month on account of the turnover in this place.

"Anything happening?" Lou said, sitting down at my desk.

I shrugged.

"You look tired," he said.

"I'm not tired," I said.

"You look hot."

"I'm not hot."

"Well it is hot," Lou said.

"It's always hot."

Lou had pasted a smile on his face, an actual certifiable smile, a first since the stroke. But it was the smile of a man keeping a secret – but not for long.

Of course Old Lou already had a secret. He wasn't allowed to drive. Declaring him impaired, the city had revoked his license. So how was he supposed to go out on calls without a car? So he drove. Risking jail and who knew what else. But a salesman without a car was like a jockey without a horse. So Lou kept on driving usually upon the roads but sometimes upon the sidewalks.

I said, "What's so funny, Lou?"

"I'm not allowed to smile?"

"There's no law."

"I'm happy, that's why I'm smiling."

"Well I'm happy that you're happy, Lou."

"I'm not allowed to be happy?"

"Sure you are."

"I'm allowed to be happy, just like the next man. Aren't you ever happy?"

"Sometimes I'm happy."

"That's the trouble with people today. Nobody's happy. Especially young people. You're a young man."

"That's what people tell me."

"Be happy while you're young."

I forgot to mention that Lou was a philosopher.

"That's good advice, Lou."

Lou's upper lip was quivering, twisting his pencil-thin mustache into something like a snarl. Another secret about Lou was that he wore a hairpiece, the most open secret in the world, since Fat Jack liked to yank it off his head and toss it around the showroom when business was slow, Lou not complaining since that kind of horseplay certified him as still one-of-the-boys. Though lately, it's true, he was getting annoyed at being the company's number one foil. Lately, in fact, Lou was getting annoyed at everything, and who could blame him?

Like any good salesman, he loved to eat; now, since the stroke, forget steak. Forget sex.

One reason I refrained from sending him out on the big calls was that it meant getting down on all fours to measure the entire house, two, sometimes three floors, and sometimes, four, including basement, if, say, it were out in Hyde Park, where Stephanie lived and the garages were more elaborate than most homes. Out there they'd carpet the trees if they could. Anyway, in Lou's condition, that could be murder, sending him out to measure a big house. Really, it could be murder.

Fat Jack used to tell me that Lou, in his prime, had been one mean son of a bitch. He used to steal other people's leads.

But in fact Harry Himself had loved that about Lou – meant he was HUNGRY.

Show me a HUNGRY salesman, Harry used to say, and I'll show you a SUCCESS.

Nobody but nobody could say HUNGRY like Harry Himself. Not even Fat Jack. The trick was to growl the word and Fat Jack was still in the barking stage, as if to prove that he still had a ways to go before he became a replica of Harry Himself. Even more, nobody but nobody could say SUCCESS like Harry Himself. HUNGRY and SUCCESS were words specially minted for Harry Himself.

"Lunch?" Lou said.

"No. You know I don't like to be with people."

"We could go to Sister's Diner."

"The businessmen go there."

"How about Stan's Deli?"

"Yuppies."

"Granger's?"

"Artsies."

"You're a regular recluse, Eli."

"I just don't like to be with people. I hate crowds anyway."

"Don't you want to be discovered, Eli?"

"As a boiler room operator?"

"As an actor. I thought you were an actor."

"Well I am. I play a role every day."

"So do I," said Lou. "So does everybody."

I told Lou if he had something to say he could say it here.

What was it about people that they needed to eat something in order to talk?

"I know you have something to tell me."

"You know me too well," he chuckled.

"We're pals."

He checked left and right for spies. "Guess what I've got in my pocket."

I gasped. I knew what he had.

"How did you get it?" I asked.

"Never mind."

"You've got to tell me."

"I've got connections. I still have friends, you know."

"This'll make you enemies."

He turned around to block the girls out of sight and showed me the printouts. These papers were a computer read-out of all the people in town and in the suburbs who had just moved in, into new expensive homes. Names, phone numbers, and addresses. A gold mine. Worth – in this business – something like $100,000, maybe more. Just the paper alone. Because these were TOP QUALITY names, every one a sure sale for a house-full of carpet, and expensive carpet.

Lou leaned over and whispered, "How many people would die for this list?"

"I can think of one."

I wasn't kidding. I knew the man who had compiled that list, good old Stone Kiley over there at Seats Galore, who also had connections, it was reputed, but of a different kind. He wouldn't be too happy to discover that someone else had his TOP QUALITY names, without paying through the nose for them, and Old Lou sure didn't have that kind of money. For months he'd been begging Fat Jack to purchase that list but, or course, Fat Jack refused on the grounds that it was too costly, number one, and that he would never deal with a man such as Stone Kiley, number two.

Stone Kiley, by the way, once had one of his own boiler room guys beaten up for walking off with a much less valuable list, according to rumor. Anything for a list. Targeting people according to location, religion and profession was the plasma of direct marketing and if you had those select names you parted with them over your dead body. The preacher who said a good name is more precious than gold was talking to all of us, but mostly to the sales department.

"Did you buy it, Lou?"

"None of your business."

He wanted to know if my girls would make the phone contacts for him.

"That would be unethical, Lou."

Lou got hot. "What business isn't unethical?"

"My business, and I'm surprised at you."

"Don't give me that, Eli. I'm as ethical as the next man."

"That's what's starting to worry me."

"I've always been an honest man – but I CAN'T KEEP UP! You can't keep up being an honest man all your life."

I stared at him. I really was surprised. But who was I to judge? Who wrote the pitch about a once-a-year sale – that went on year-round? What about the salesmen who discounted the carpet $700 and then tacked that same amount to the cost of installation before the customer knew what hit him or her? You committed larceny all the time but you didn't even know it because they called it doing business.

"I need this," Lou said.

He needed it, he said, if for no other reason than to show the world that he was still Lou Emmett, the Lou Emmett of old. Lou Emmett wasn't dead yet. He said he knew the talk that went on behind his back. He knew the pity. He knew the ridicule. He knew the "dead salesman walking" joke and even knew that he was a stand-in for Willie Loman. "Nobody does a man any favors," he said. "A man has to do for himself. That's my philosophy."

"Or your life."

"So you won't do it for me?"

"Do me a favor, Lou. Give that list back."

"All right. I'll make the calls myself. They don't even have to be verified they're so good."

"Give it back, Lou."

"I can't. I'll do what I have to do. No hard feelings," he said, getting up. "Pals?"

"Pals," I said as he shuffled out.

Mona said, "What was that all about?"
"Lou is going into business for himself."
"What kind of business?"
"The suicide business."

Chapter 11

Fat Jack was on the phone. I could tell by his voice he had big bad news for me.

First I asked him if he had shut off the air conditioner, which he had, not to save money, but as punishment.

"It's ninety-five degrees up here and my girls are melting."

The walls were sweating, the floors were buckling and the phones were beginning to soak.

"Let them get me leads for my starving men and I'll turn it back on."

"You shut the air off for that?"

"I can't afford the air your girls are costing me, Eli. Air costs money."

"Air?"

But true, air costs money. Breathing is expensive.

"The accountant was just here. Harry Himself is on my back. He's thinking of bringing in an efficiency expert to take inventory of people like you."

Life, breath by breath, pound for pound, is measured on the scales of finance.

"That wouldn't be the end of the world."

"No, but it might be the end of your job."

"That still wouldn't be the end of the world. Listen Fat Jack, turn the air back on or I'm coming down."

I heard him regaling and then I heard the air click back on.

"Happy now?"

"Yes."

"But it's about to get hotter for you, Eli."

"I'm not in a good mood today, Fat Jack."

"Oh, so I guess you don't care that a silver Jaguar just pulled up in front of the showroom. My, my. I wonder whose car that could be!"

Of course it was Stephanie's.

"Getting hotter, Eli?"

So he wasn't kidding after all? Can it be? No, I refused to get snared in. Ever since it sort of ended with us – her going off to California – Fat Jack had me running to the windows and to the phones at least once a week to chase after a phantom Stephanie, so that by now I was immune to the trick, practically. He loved to play tricks, Fat Jack did, and he also loved Stephanie, in a brotherly way, and had worked very hard, in his clumsy manner, to bring us together, and now that we were apart he blamed the whole thing on me, frequently saying, "Stephanie Eatons don't grow on trees."

Which I already knew.

"That could have been you in that Jaguar," he said, "and everything that goes with it – and I mean everything. She could have BOUGHT you Broadway."

True.

"I know you're pulling my leg."

"Oh yeah? Look out the window. I told you she was coming. Go on, you yutz."

"You want leads? Let me get back to work."

"You mean back to sleep."

"Up here it's the same thing."

"Eli, you really blew it with her. You could have been a KING."

"Goodbye."

"What a waste!"

"Goodbye."

"I ought to come up there and slap you around."

"Goodbye."

"Here she comes now. God she's gorgeous. A yutz like you doesn't deserve this."

"Goodbye."

"I'll send her up soon as I'm done talking to her. I'm gonna tell her how sick you've been since she left."

"Don't you dare."

"You mean you believe she's here?"

"No," I said.

"Goodbye," and he hung up.

"You two," Mona said. "You're like a couple of kids."

"He says Stephanie's here."

"Is she?"

"Of course not."

Of course I wasn't about to look out the window, either.

Chapter 12

But here she was, Stephanie Eaton, debutante, heiress, princess, gorgeous as ever, stunning as always, dark hair gloriously wild, shaggy, untamed, face full of that big warm smile that ignited those steamy eyes. Tall, erect, elegant, even majestic, leaning somewhat stylishly on her shoulder bag. Whispery in that High Society way of hers; what breeding! Long but soft strides as though always treading on velvet. Hers was a life of grand entrances. Spiral staircases followed her around. Yachts were in dock for her, limos waiting, jets revved up, sought by poets, favored by kings, pursued by princes. But here, she was my Stephanie. She was Fat Jack's Stephanie. She was Mona's Stephanie. She was our Stephanie.

Stephanie Eaton – there was nothing like her today. Go back to Bathsheba or Ava Gardner to find her equal.

She and Mona fell into an embrace, Mona exclaiming, "I knew you'd come back."

"I've missed you."

She looked around.

"Nothing's changed," she said.

Mona took that as an affront. What did Stephanie think we were: quaint?

"Oh much has changed since you were here last," Mona said.

"I'm sure. What I meant was – it's still here. Everything's still here."

What she meant was, I was still here, not exactly a compliment.

* * *

We got into her car. She drove as if she owned the roads. She shifted gears – up, down, sideways – with the gusto and expertise of a Mario Andretti and asked me if I wanted to take the wheel. "I love to shift gears," she said, casting me a naughty side-glance, which turned my heart.

"You love to shift gears?"

"It's so sensual."

She'd never talked like that before...before California.

They loved to shift gears out there because it was so sensual. Hmmm.

We headed for a "quick bite" to Sugar n' Spice on Reading Road, quick because she didn't really have too much time. (Even when the going between us was good she always had places to go. The rich always have places to go. The rest of us stay put.) Sugar n' Spice was more than just a restaurant; it was now a nostalgic monument to our romantic past, for it was here, eight months ago, a few weeks before she took off for California – here she had proposed marriage, and here I had declined.

I had wanted to marry her, of course, more than anything, except for the terms, which were not to my liking in that I'd end up having to work for her father, who owned half of Cincinnati through inheritance alone. Very old money. I'd have to give up my independence, my individuality, my freedom, my dreams of returning to New York and becoming an actor. I'd be suffocated, trapped, caged. The socialite Stephanie Eaton – I could always keep track of her by simply turning to the Society Pages of *The Cincinnati Enquirer* – would not countenance a boiler room manager for a husband. A carpet salesman. That was not only embarrassing for a future, but also humbling for a past. What would the neighbors – the Pews and Vanderbilts – say?

Eight months ago, right here, in perhaps the same booth we were now sharing at Sugar n' Spice, she had sighed: "Oh Eli, let's get married." This was some moment. We had spent a hot night in her apartment, no outright lovemaking of course, but she had gone down to her bra and panties and almost let me touch her here and there, Brahms and Beethoven for the music. I'd gotten her into classical music as she got me into painting.

"Married?" I said.

"Yes," she said. "Let's get married."

"You and me?"

She laughed.

"Let's do it right now, before other things get in the way."

Such as her parents sending her off to California, which they were proposing to do, possibly to get her away from me. Her parents, mother especially, was no fan of mine. Stephanie could do better, and actually I agreed. She could do much better. Of all her suitors, surely I ranked at zero. Stephanie had said they were serious about shipping her off to college. Marriage would beat them at their game. Headstrong as she was, she was always in conflict with them. I figured she had set her mind on marriage merely to get even with them.

"This minute?" I said.

"Don't let it pass," she said.

"Elope?"

"Blood test – everything! Tonight. Now."

She had a life. I had nothing but dreams. I'd only be bringing her futility. That wouldn't be fair.

"Don't let it pass," Stephanie repeated, back then, months ago at Sugar n' Spice.

I was about to say yes, in fact I did say yes in my head, but instead this came out:

"Only to have your dad go chasing after us, maybe annul the marriage."

"Oh they'll be angry at first. But they'll come around. They'll have to forgive me. I'm their daughter."

They'd come around all right, put me to work in the COMPANY BUSINESS.

"My career?"

I meant acting, not boiler room.

"Daddy will help."

Exactly what I was afraid of. What about my freedom of choice?

"Eli. I love you."

Again I said yes, but this came out: "Let's give it a few days."

She leaned back and the warm gaze left her eyes.

"So I guess it's California," she said.

She was using me to keep from going to California?

"I didn't say no. I just said let's think about it," – but she wasn't listening anymore.

Later that night I thought about it and realized my mistake, an enormous once-in-a-lifetime blunder.

A few days later we were back at Sugar n' Spice and I said, "Let's get married, Stephanie. Now."

Did she get a kick out of that one!

"Oh, Eli," she sighed, "that moment has passed."

* * *

So that was eight months ago and, except for night and day, I never brooded about it again.

* * *

"Why do you call him Fat Jack?" asked the new Stephanie Eaton, who had gone to California and come back.

"Because that's his name."

"I think he's sweet."

"Fat Jack?"

"You know he means well."

"You look terrific, Stephanie."

"I do? You've never told me that before."

"Sure I have."

"You've never told me I was beautiful."

"I thought you knew."

She smiled that sensational smile and touched my hand. "Women have to be told. At least once a day, if possible."

"That wouldn't be too hard," I said.

She shot me a look of surprise. "You've changed."

"How?"

"You've become more romantic. I like it."

She had ordered her usual toasted English muffin; I was having the apple pie a la mode.

"Same apple pie a la mode," she said.

"Same English muffin for the lady," I said.

We were getting along, but there was always something else...something sure to come.

I asked how long she'd been back from California, expecting something like hours, a day at the most.

Obviously she had rushed here straight from the airport.

"Two weeks," she said blithely.

I gulped and said, "I can't blame you for not calling sooner. I know how difficult it is to pick up a phone."

"Oh, Eli. We're not going to quarrel, are we? Aren't you happy to see me?"

"Thrilled."

"You can be so exasperating," she said. "Why do women always have to prove themselves to men?"

She sighed. One thing about Stephanie Eaton. Nobody could sigh like her. In a sighing contest she was the one to put the money on.

Now she sighed – "Eli, I have a favor to ask."

"Shoot."

"I need your advice. You've always been so good with advice."

I could feel something coming.

"I have?"

"Yes. You've always been so sensible."

Oh. Like when I refused to marry her that very instant?

That moment has passed.

How many times a day had I lived that line?

"I'm not so sensible," I insisted.

"Eli," she sighed. "I may be in love again."

I tried to hide back a smirk, though I deserved one for winning her back. I congratulated myself on my patience.

"Who's the lucky guy?" I asked, barely suppressing my delight.

"A professor I met at UCLA."

Was that a Sherman tank that had just crushed over me, or could mere words crush you like that?

"What's wrong, Eli? You look sick."

I said nothing for about five minutes.

"You want my advice?" I finally said.

"Why yes."

"Now I'm your brother? Your FRIEND?"

"Oh forget it, Eli," she huffed. "Forget I said anything. Who's that new girl in the boiler room by the way?"

"I'm FLABBERGASTED," I said, borrowing one of her high class phrases.

"No you're not."

"What sort of advice did you want?"

"Are you sure?"

"WHAT SORT OF ADVICE DID YOU WANT?"

"Don't shout," she said, and then, remembering she was back home in Cincinnati, she added the "please."

"What sort of advice did you want?"

"Well...he's nice and all that, a PhD, but he's so wild."

"A wild college professor."

"Yes."

"A wild PhD."

"Yes."

"You used to say I was wild."

"Well you are. But not like him."

"Amazing how you rich girls go for WILD."

"Please don't shout."

"I'm not wild enough? You want wild? I'll show you wild."

"You're making a scene."

"Well that's wild, isn't it?"

"That's not what I mean, now please stop it," she said.

"What does he do that's so WILD? Does he drive fast? Does he PEEL RUBBER?"

"You don't understand."

"Does he pick you up and throw you into the pool? At parties does he put a lampshade on his head?"

"I want to leave. People are staring."

"Does he lap up food like a dog? Watch me."

"Don't. Please."

But I had already bent down gobbling the ice cream off the apple pie.

"That's enough, Eli. Now we can never come back."

And maybe that's what I was trying to do, put a period at the end of a sentence that refused to quit. A thousand times we had ended it, and that many times she had done something, said something, whispered something, SIGHED something, to offer a flicker of hope and that's what I had been living on, and dying on. After I calmed down, and we were waiting for the check, I told her about the new girl.

"Sonja's her name."

"She gives me the willies."

"Join the club."

"What do you mean?"

"She's psychic."

"Well she gives me the creeps."

"How? Did she say anything to you? Look at you funny?"

"That's the point. She didn't look at me at all."

"Hmm."

"Usually, when a person walks into a room, you look. It's instinct. But she didn't look. At least not with her eyes. But I felt her."

So I told her all about Sonja, and about how Sonja might be a danger to her.

"What can she do to me?"

"I don't know. But she may be insane."

"I'm not going to worry about it," Stephanie said.

"But it's something to think about."

"So why don't you fire her?"

"She knows where I live."

"She probably knows where I live, too," Stephanie said, showing a trace of concern. "What's her problem?"

"She hates the fact that I'm in love with you. At least she thinks I'm in love with you."

Now Stephanie softened. She smiled.

"Are you?" she sighed. "Fat Jack thinks you're still in love with me."

"What does he know?"

"Fat Jack said you were sick while I was gone."

"I'm also sick when you're here."

She laughed. Then she sighed. "Oh, Eli."

"Do you still love me?" I dared.

"I care about you. Very much."

What the hell did that mean? Was that something new I'd take home with me? Was there a space between CARE and LOVE? How much? Did VERY MUCH bring it closer to the real thing? Was love a magic word or could two people make a life out of CARING VERY MUCH?

"That wild college professor, does he remind you of me?"

"Yes he does. He's handsome."

"But more handsome."

"I didn't say that."

"Smarter."

"No, you're just as smart, in your own way."

"Wittier?"

"No. In fact you're much funnier."

"So he's only wilder? That's all I've got to beat?"

"You don't have to beat anything, Eli. Just stay as you are. Have you found a facsimile for me?"

"No, Stephanie, you're one of a kind, as we say in the rug business."

"You think of me as a carpet?" she laughed happily.

"I think of everything as carpet. It gets that way."

"What sort of carpet am I?"

"Oriental."

"Is that the best?"

"Supposed to last a lifetime."

She was entirely mellow now, and not in the California mode.

"I guess it was crude of me to bring up another guy. Only I thought you had forgotten all about me. You never wrote."

"Neither did you."

"You never called."

"Neither did you."

"I was sure you had found someone else," she said.

"I was sure you hadn't."

She sighed. "I like it here. This is OUR place, isn't it, Eli?"

"You said we're never coming back."

"That's because you were acting so foolish."

"I was only being wild."

She laughed, then turned serious. "I saw that green ribbon on your desk. The one I once left in your apartment."

"I didn't know I still had it," I said.

"I saw it on your desk, Eli. Don't be ashamed of being sentimental. I'm glad I'm still in your heart. But life..."

"Uh-oh..."

"But life goes on," she said.

Chapter 13

The last person I wanted to see when I got back was Old Lou. Always after a get-together with Stephanie I wanted to be alone. Especially if it was a good one, so I could extract the gold, and especially if it was a bad one, where I could sort through the wreckage. This time, on the wreckage front, I was left with LIFE GOES ON. What a thing to say!

Even worse than Lou at a moment like this was Fat Jack. I had to pass the showroom on my way up.

Fat Jack was giving a speech.

Saying: "The most important thing in life is SELLING."

He spotted me trying to sneak through the crowd. "This is for you too, Eli."

Phil Coleman and the other salesmen smiled. They suspected I wasn't one of them.

They thought I was a spy.

Maybe I was a spy to the extent that I loved to watch people and considered myself not above or beneath them, but merely detached, an observer, as any good actor had to be – and frankly, it amazed me that not all people were actors. What else made any sense? In my New York days I worked with a waiter named Big Stan who said he wasn't, WAS NOT waiting on tables as a means to support an acting career. He was a waiter because he WANTED TO BE A WAITER. That was his profession. He was proud of his profession. Was it possible, therefore, that there were bus drivers who wanted to be bus drivers, and ditto for cabbies, construction workers, janitors, window washers, maids, valets, insect EXTERMINA-TORS, hatters, plumbers, carpenters – weren't they all just biding their time until their agents gave them a call? Weren't they all spies? Obviously not. I had it all wrong. Which was good. It would be a world without food and water if we all pursued the same task. Fortunately we all sorted ourselves out, like bees and ants, and went scurrying into different jobs and professions for the general GOOD. We thought we were individuals but all we did was supply the demand.

As for me, nature had decreed that there was a greater need for boiler room managers than for actors.

* * *

Fat Jack said every man here was behind on his quota... "And that's the problem. The fact that you're HERE. The fact that you're here means that you're not THERE. Outside. Selling." It was understood that walk-in trade was never as lucrative as OUTSIDE; walk-in customers were usually in the market for something to cover the hallway – a lousy rug! Morris Silver could handle that by himself, if he wasn't in the middle of a tall story. In the carpet business all that counted was wall-to-wall. "I want HUNGRY salesmen," Fat Jack said.

Fat Jack was a terrific orator, maybe not of the Shakespearean cut, but he was a terrific speaker; you could tell that by the way he held his audience, in this case the sales force, spellbound. Nobody moved. Nobody said a word. If not spellbound, then every man here certainly was asleep, Morris Silver grumbling, "Same old garbage."

Hot shot Phil Coleman whispered back, "Show some respect for the young."

"Yeah the young," said Morris. "You young guys. Yeah, you really know what it's all about."

Phil Coleman laughed. "You're just jealous."

"Yeah I'm jealous. I'm so jealous."

What I liked about Morris Silver was how he disagreed with everything you said by agreeing with everything you said, a rare and wonderful skill. Like someone would say to Fat Jack, "That's a nice suit you've got on." Morris Silver would say, "Yeah, that's some nice suit you got. Yeah, real nice." Or someone would make a complimentary remark about the President of the United States and Morris Silver would say, "Oh yeah, he's a champ. A real jewel." In his own way, though, Morris Silver was a great thinker, equal to, say, Freud, as when he once told me, in fewer words than Freud ever used – in fact he summed it all up for Freud when he said, "For you guys, what more is there to life besides pussy?"

* * *

When I got upstairs Lou was already sitting at my desk. I told him the most important thing in life was selling. I said Fat Jack had challenged me to come up with something more important, like maybe ACTING, WRITING, LEARING, PHILOSOPHY, CULTURE in general, but I couldn't come up with anything.

"You're not being sarcastic, are you?"

No I wasn't. I was becoming a believer.

"Maybe Fat Jack is right," Lou said. "If you don't believe selling is the most important thing, maybe you shouldn't be here. If you don't believe in what you're doing..."

Fair enough. He had me there. True, I did not believe in what I was doing. Chalk one up for Lou.

I said, "What's the matter, Lou? You seem down in the dumps."

It wasn't like Lou to come at me so directly, saying, in effect, if I didn't like it here I shouldn't be here, and frankly I was hurt and insulted. We were pals. But of course we weren't pals. We were pals so long as he needed me and I needed him. He needed me for leads and I needed him for...who knew? What was he to me except a salesman, a pretty mediocre salesman at that, and not the most pleasant individual, prone to outbursts of temper, against others, at real or imagined slights, understandable, to be sure, for his age and in his condition, and maybe that was it, I was scoring points being nice to a man nobody else had patience for, I was being GOOD. For all I knew, I didn't even like him – and he didn't like me. But we'd never find out because we were kind of thrown in together. The more pathetic he became, the more I stuck by him. Maybe, lacking any real purpose here, I had made Lou my purpose. Maybe. Or maybe I was performing, world's greatest actor that I was, using the boiler room as a stage, expecting applause.

If it can't be Broadway or Hollywood, it'll have to be the boiler room. Let it be the boiler room.

Anyway, it wasn't like him to attack me.

Once in a while he'd say I was a fish out of water.

But that was the extent of his nastiness.

"I'm not in a bad mood," he said.

But Lou, it turned out, was not only in a bad mood. He was in bad trouble. Someone had contacted him about that list of QUALITY customers he had purloined, and wanted it back, of course – pronto. Lou had refused. But whoever had called him had threatened him. Threatened to do harm if he didn't return that list. Lou, circling his wagons, had threatened to make Xerox copies of that list, said he would distribute these duplicates to every salesman in town, rendering the list useless, turning, therefore, gold into dust.

"Are you crazy?"

"I've already started going out on calls," he said, chuckling, and I should have gathered as much from that new bow tie he was sporting, not to mention that carnation in his lapel, and his sweet-smelling breath all of a sudden and the cologne which announced him a mile off, all signs of a salesman back in action!

"From that list?" I asked.

He was beaming. "Made a six thousand dollar sale yesterday."

That was six times more than he had ever made from the best of my leads.

"Didn't Fat Jack wonder where you got the lead?"

Lou said nothing for a while and I couldn't imagine what he was holding back.

"I told him you gave it to me."

Calmly, I told Lou never to do that again.

"I was only making you look good."

"Don't make me look good, Lou."

"I thought I was doing you a favor."

"Don't do me favors. Not these. What's gotten into you?"

"Survival."

"That's no answer."

"How about SALES? That's the answer. Fat Jack keeps saying it and you keep not believing it but that's why we're here, Eli! We're here to sell. In case you didn't know it, I'm a salesman. Selling is what I do. I don't sell, I don't exist."

"You can't be that desperate."

"Who isn't?"

"Lou – they're going to come after you."

"Who?"

"The boys who called you, Lou, and who were they, by the way?"

"It was just one guy."

"Who?"

"Some guy."

He wouldn't tell.

What I couldn't tell him was that if he kept going out on wall-to-wall jobs, that by itself would finish him. I'd been out with bigger, stronger and healthier guys and watched them huffing and puffing and nearly collapsing from the rigors of measuring – whereas Lou was extended to the max simply to negotiate his way across the showroom.

"I appreciate your concern," Lou said.

"I thought I knew you, Lou."

"People are full of surprises," he said.

Mona didn't know what was going on, of course, so as Lou got up to leave, she said: "I think I have a lead for you, Lou. I can't verify till next week, when her husband comes back from..."

"That's okay, Mona. Take your time. I'm in no hurry."

After he left, Mona said, "Was that Lou talking, or was it my imagination?"

"He's not hungry anymore, Mona. At least not for our leads."

"Why not?"

"You don't want to know."

* * *

Sonja the Psychic said, "So that was Stephanie."

She was being sugary, for starters.

"Yes it was," I said.

"I know I promised to be good, but mind if I say something?"

"I hope it's nice."

"Yes it is. You're too good for her. She doesn't appreciate you."

"Thanks for the advice."

"You deserve better."

"Thanks."

"She thinks she's hot stuff."

"That's enough, Sonja."

"Don't you know what she's really like?"

"Yes I do."

"Men are so blind. What will it take to open your eyes?"

Chapter 14

I was in my apartment in Mount Adams. The stars were out and the Reds were in LA. They usually sank in the West. Upstairs Kevin Ivy was humping his secretary, Felice. (She was black, his wife was white, very white.) I heard her climax. If it's Felice, it must be Wednesday. Felice was ferocious in bed. Not that I knew this firsthand, so to speak, but it was enough just to listen to her. She made wonderful sounds and she never failed to ignite me when she finally let out that big yell. You couldn't help but get turned-on vicariously. After it was all done she'd walk down the stairs, unsteadily for she usually climaxed in succession, sometimes three in a row (is that a record?) and offer me an inviting smile as if the two of us had shared something as well.

Kevin was a lawyer and so damned proper. All his friends were lawyers. Even judges. Every other night, except Wednesdays, dozens of his proper friends spread themselves out upstairs, drinking beer, including the redhead Gloria who'd always come down when I was alone, rip off her clothes and rape me. She bit. She was a biter. That was one way I

was sure who was in bed with me. I could understand biting in the heat of passion, but she took a nip
sometimes when it was all over and I had started to
doze, or was walking her to the door, and she did
complain about that, about my napping, but anyway,
I kept telling her to quit the damned biting but she
said it helped her. She needed it for arousal. She said
I ought to try it too, in which case, I said, we ought to
get down on all fours and wag our tails. She always
climaxed and it was always good sex for me, too,
though I didn't know and didn't want to know a thing
about her, hardly even knew what she looked like
with the lights out all the time. She was a redhead,
most probably. Maybe she was married. We'd come
together, she'd get dressed, and leave and get proper
again. Gloria was a lawyer. She kept imploring me to
enter her anally, which I'd never do, first of all
because it was against the LAW. This was Cincinnati
where they fined you and sometimes arrested you
for JAYWALKING. Imagine sodomy or something. I
wondered what Gloria was like in court.

The other neighbor upstairs, by the way, was a
guy named Malcolm Wayworth. Talk about proper,
and UPSTANDING. He was an insurance salesman,
short, wore a crew cut, and nobody in all of
Cincinnati was more polite than he was, and that
was saying something. In a polite contest, Malcolm
Wayworth took the prize. He never failed to smile
and say good morning, or good evening. He was
married to a sweet, petite lady you almost never saw,
but when you did, she was hiding a black eye or

something. Every now and then you'd hear noises upstairs.

They didn't live directly above me, that would be Kevin Ivy, so the noises must have been pretty loud, and the sounds were of violence. Couldn't be, though, could it, that that upstanding citizen was beating his wife? An INSURANCE SALESMAN? Stephanie had been here once when that racket was going on upstairs and she wanted to know what it was, and I said they were probably moving furniture.

Listen, she said, I think I hear a woman. He's BEATING HER! Aren't we going to do something? So we went upstairs, knocked on the door, and his wife answered. She was black and blue and her eyes were very red. I asked if everything was all right and she said yes it was. Malcolm came to the door as upstanding as ever and apologized for the commotion, though never saying what it was. When we were downstairs again Stephanie was distraught over the fact that we were so HELPLESS. We couldn't do anything. "Don't you feel we should have done something?" she said. I shrugged. I said whatever had to be done I was ready to do. But there was nothing to do. Even the WOMAN denied that she was being beaten and she'd probably deny it to the police, all the way to court. I didn't say (from my own experience) what could happen once you interfered between two people. To be your brother's keeper was fine, I was all for it, but it wasn't that easy. Anyway, you can't go knocking on every door. Anything can be going on inside, kissing or killing. Stephanie said, "Well I think it's OUTRAGEOUS that we can't do anything to stop that man." I agreed. I said if I ever caught him in the act...but I never would of course, and that poor woman would go on getting beat up. I knew that, Stephanie knew that, Malcolm knew that, his wife knew that, but that was how it was, something like the law of the jungle, yes, even here in Cincinnati. Stephanie made me promise to catch her alone one day and ask her. Which I did. I tried. I said, "Does your husband...Is your husband...Are you?" She stared me in the face, quite affectionately, and said, "I'll manage," and walked away.

Stephanie, when I reported this back to her, wasn't comforted. She didn't come right out and say so but I could detect this much, she was annoyed that I wasn't taking action. Right, I ought to go upstairs and punch him out for ALLEGEDLY beating his wife, have him call the cops, have her say her husband never touched her, and have the cops check my records. Or, go in there, throw him a punch, and kill him – which could happen. It wasn't like the movies. In real life you hit somebody, it could be lethal. Yes it could. So you had to be careful, very careful, before you became your brother's or your sister's keeper. Domestic violence is tricky business. Ask any officer of the law. This much Stephanie did say, "I'm SURPRISED that you can live here under these conditions." As if conditions were perfect elsewhere. Maybe in Hyde Park – and I was willing to bet there were a few wife beaters there, too. Stephanie said, "And he looks so meek, that evil little man!" I said that's the thing about evil, it usually comes with a false front. But she couldn't get over how HELPLESS we were.

* * *

I was watching the Reds against the Dodgers. How I hated those Dodgers. Los Angeles. California. Where PhD college professors were WILD. They were losing, these Reds, to those wild PhD Dodgers. They were down three zip at the bottom of the first and the Dodgers still had men on base, when the phone rang and it was Stephanie, saying, late as it was, she wanted to come over. Would I mind? Of course I wouldn't mind.

"I have a surprise for you," she said.

She sounded terrific. Once in a while she got that way, so warm, so giving, so loving, so uninhibited, no tricks, no games; if only I could bottle it for safekeeping. She simply let herself go, at these times, and I wondered if it was something within me, something I communicated to win this sort of affection. If so, what was I doing wrong the other times? Most of the time. Why couldn't she always be this perfect? Why couldn't I always be perfect?

The big question for me was this: What made it click then but not now, or now but not then?

Stephanie often said that love is chemistry. Well, chemistry is an exact science. Love is not an exact science.

"You sound happy."

"You know those paintings I've been working on all these years..."

"The ones you refuse to show me."

"Well I've decided to show them to you."

"Great."

"You won't be too critical, will you?"

They were on giant canvases, these paintings. I asked her how she was going to bring them over.

"I've already strapped them to the roof of my car."

"But that's ridiculous. Why don't I go over to your house?"

She'd feel self-conscious about them with her parents around...and besides, it was very late.

She said, "You know what I've come to realize?"

"What?"

"That you've been the inspiration for every painting I've ever done. I even drew something of you."

She said she hadn't painted a thing in California, but couldn't stop since she'd been back in Cincinnati.

"Back to you," she said.

I was touched. I really was.

She asked me if I still loved her.

Trick question?

"Yes I do."

"Because I think you should only show paintings to people who love you. Paintings and poems are like dreams. Only the interpretation counts. Are you watching the ballgame? Stay put, I'll be right over."

Only the interpretation counts.

I stepped outside to behold the hills of Cincinnati, seven of them, like Rome, Cincinnati's sister city. Cincinnati, in fact, was named after the Roman general Cincinnatus who retired from the battlefield to take up the passive life of a farmer, which also held true for the town to this day, passive and tranquil (except for a riot here and there). I suddenly loved this town and this entire universe very much. All it took was one phone call. Back when we were perfect together we shared King Solomon's haiku – "I am my beloved's my beloved is mine." It started to rain. I went inside, took a shower, dressed up in fresh clothes and carefully combed my hair. I watched some more of the ballgame but wasn't paying close attention. Futility, like these Reds in LA, can be contagious. Then I went back and combed my hair again. I decided to shave. Then I combed my hair again. This time WILD.

I was wondering how we could hold these moments. This had to be the first discussion between us in ages where everything had clicked and I wondered what could happen to mess it up. We were so good at messing things up. What would it be this time? Always it was something unforeseen.

It was taking her a long time to get here. I turned the sound down on the TV and put on some Brahms. I hadn't been able to listen to music for eight months. Now I leaned back and let it sweep me along and take me places, like that country home of hers in which we had spent a magical 12 hours, even walking along a stream and discussing the children we would one day raise, me a famous actor, she a great painter. Now there – that had been a perfect day, from beginning to end.

Even when anticipating the best, I was invariably on edge awaiting her arrival, so to pass the time I thought I'd go out and bring us back some beer, though I didn't drink the stuff, she did, had developed a renewed taste for beer ever since California, naturally, and I found myself wondering what else went along with beer, but anyway, I decided to step out to 7-11, a bit of a walk, and it was raining. I taped a note to the door in case she got here before me with her paintings. I figured her showing me her paintings was a big moment for us, renewal, rebirth, salvation.

Least I could do was get some beer and maybe some cookies and things.

It was raining all right but I didn't take an umbrella. Real men don't use umbrellas. As I started walking in the rain Claudius, Kevin's dachshund, began to follow me and Kevin yelled out from the window that it was all right for his dog to accompany me, since he, Kevin, didn't want to go out in the rain to walk him. I loved the dog anyway. He sniffed everything along the way and I was afraid he might get run over, but he was a smart dog and did not venture out into the street.

I picked up a 6-pack and as the clerk rang it up the machine, not the clerk, said, "Thank you. Have a nice day."

We now leave it to machines to express courtesy.

When I got back I brushed my teeth again. Stephanie wasn't here yet.

Kevin asked me where his dog was.

"Dog?"

I never walked a dog before so I guess I forgot that when you took them out you had to bring them back.

"Oh shit!" He ran out yelling for his dog. "In the rain," I heard him say.

In the rain?

In the rain?

Son of a bitch, it's raining.

It's RAINING!

* * *

Dad called to ask if he was disturbing me.

"They get killed out there," he groaned.

Dad was an ardent fan of the Reds. Make that passionate. Better yet, irrational. He never watched them on TV, old-timer that he was, or read about them in the papers; only listened to them on the radio and faithfully kept score of each play, as he had done nigh on 50 years. He still thought all the players were white. (Pissin' and moanin' was how it was in Cincinnati over these Reds. Johnny Wilder, the guy in the stock room back at Harry's Carpet City, swore that his ulcers came from the Reds.)

The high point of Dad's life was when Cincinnati's Johnny Vander Meer pitched back-to-back no-hitters a million years ago. (A feat never duplicated.) The low point was when, during an open tryout for kids, I misjudged a fly ball in the outfield, which wasn't nearly as small and tidy as it appears on TV. A major league outfield is IMMENSE, is like WYOMING, and in this vastness you were supposed to spot a tiny ball, run it down, and catch it, too?

"You know what it means when the Reds lose," Dad now said.

"You don't have to tell me."

But he would.

"It means bad luck."

He really believed that and he even had evidence to support his view that when the Reds went bad, everything went bad. Mother died three weeks after they dumped Tony Perez. Nothing could dissuade Dad from his belief that there was a connection. Dad had predicted disaster after that misguided trade, and not just for Cincinnati, but for all America as well, and yes, the entire WORLD. (The Reds never recovered, as if cursed.)

Subsequent wars, famines, economic plunges, earthquakes, tornadoes, typhoons, mudslides, plane crashes, hijackings, kidnappings, drug epidemics, fires, explosions, hostage-taking, public decapitations, honor killings, jihads, riots, rebellions, terrorism, school shootings and a general worldwide restiveness – proved him prophetic.

"We need pitching," he said.

"We need hitting," I said.

We never talked about the real things, about things that really touched us, using, instead, baseball to express our emotions, though Dad had no emotions. For example, Dad was dying of cancer, and from the day they discovered it, Dad only bitched about the Reds.

He had not been the kind of guy you'd talk to about your job, your career, your ambitions, your love life, your successes, your failures, your fears, your FEELINGS. Such stuff was too remote for him. He had done his job. Provided the semen. The rest was up to you. And if you needed help, there was always the Reds bullpen in the late innings.

Could I ever tell Dad that I maybe slew a man in New York? He didn't even understand why I went to New York, or why ANYBODY went to New York. Cincinnati was all he knew, except for a stint in France in World War Two, which had no affect on him at all, didn't broaden him as travel and adventure were supposed to. He came back, obviously the same way he left. International, cosmopolitan were not words you'd use to describe Dad. (Or Cincinnati.) He was a regular guy. Still wore suspenders. Never went to church, and he was a religious man, in his own way. But he never went to church. Never went to parties and when the Reds won the World Series that year, that wasn't Dad jumping up and down in Fountain Square.

(He stopped going to church after Mom died and stopped being formally religious after Mom died. He had always been a man of teetering faith and scoffed at church sermons as mumbo jumbo. He refused to visit Mom's grave as that would mean she was really

103

gone. He had to be coaxed to the funeral. He stared out the window, waiting.)

"I'll be over tomorrow night for about an hour," I said.

He took that as a warning.

"Make it around nine."

The game came on at 10.

* * *

She arrived as if blown from a shipwreck. She was soaked from the rain, face dripping water and make-up, tears bubbling in her eyes.

"They're gone," she said. "Everything's gone."

She was sobbing. She needed comforting but to take her in my arms would be cheap, and what is there to say at a stricken time like this? Some people have it worse? Thank God you've got your health? You'll paint again? You're rich, you're young, you're beautiful, you've got your whole life ahead of you – what's a couple of lousy paintings? This is no tragedy, merely a setback. But this wasn't the time to bring that up, especially after she said that every work of art is a testimony to perfection, therefore perfect, in the eyes of the artist, and irreplaceable.

But it hadn't happened as I thought, for she HAD wrapped the paintings in burlap and tied them down securely on the roof of her car – or so she thought. "I didn't count on the wind," she said. "As soon as it started to rain – I was on the expressway – I gunned it, going at least seventy." Knowing her, probably ninety. "I saw the clouds. I thought I could beat the downpour. Then I started feeling vibrations. I thought it was from my driving so fast. Then the wind came. Then one of the canvasses dropped and started dangling on the windshield. Oh, Eli...I was terrified. I slowed down to pull over and another painting fell off to my right side, then my left side. By the time I pulled over they were scattered all over Reading Road. I was so stupid. I tried to chase them down, until I realized, what's the use, in all this rain. They're gone. Everything's gone. Oh, Eli."

I put on my raincoat, grabbed her and said, "Let's go."

She said it was futile but I said we had to give it a try.

I drove. She was too shaken to do anything. We got to the spot where it had all happened, walking along the side of the highway under what had become a thunderstorm. She was right. Everything was gone. Not quite. Far off, near the Exit, I had spotted a couple of the canvasses but they were so shredded from the wind and the rain that I thought it best not to draw her attention to them; the sight of them would only make it worse for her.

We drove back to my apartment, drenched.

"I was so sure I had them tied down right," she said.

"How could they have come loose? Did you drive off after you tied them down?"

"No. I went back in the house to call you, remember?"

"Then?"

"Then I did a few other things."

"For how long?"

"About a half hour. Why?"

"I don't know. Could somebody have tampered with the cords?"

"Impossible. You know my driveway. You can't miss any car driving up. What are you getting at, Eli?"

"Just playing detective."

"It's nobody's fault but my own. Now everything's ruined."

"Not everything."

"EVERYTHING."

I said nothing. There was no reaching out to her at a time like this.

"This was supposed to be such a beautiful night. OUR night. We haven't had many of those, lately."

"No we haven't."

"It's like an omen."

"There's no such thing as omens. An accident happened. That's the beginning and the end."

"It's not the paintings anymore," she said. "It's – EVERYTHING. Everything seems to go wrong with us."

I'd never seen her sink so low, in such despair. Never thought she had it in her, this daughter of fortune. I'd never seen her as anything but proud and regal and high spirited. This wasn't like her to be so bruised and afflicted. Just then – it happened to be Wednesday – Felice upstairs was having her big bang climax for Kevin. We both listened and I must have smiled as I always did when Felice gave up her fireworks.

Stephanie stiffened. "You're laughing?"

"Not at this. Upstairs."

She bolted for the door.

"Stephanie, please..."

She calmed down and gave me the benefit of the doubt, but it was a bad moment, that inadvertent smile of mine.

"I'm sorry," she said.

"Believe me, I'm as upset as you are about your paintings."

Was I? I was upset that she was upset, but not about the paintings.

"Everything seems to go wrong, period," she said. "Never mind the paintings."

"The wind wasn't that strong," I said.

"Yes it was. Don't forget I was driving. Fast. That's wind. I'm going home."

She said it was WONDERFUL and VALIANT of me to go out with her to try and save her paintings.

Actually it wasn't the paintings I had been trying to save; it was us.

I felt, as I usually did around her, that I wasn't doing enough. I was letting her down. Was all this my fault?

She was standing by the door.

"I wish you'd stay," I said.

"I can't."

"Why not?"

"I can't. You know I can't. I can imagine how I look."

"You can take a bath here."

She offered a smile.

"You'd like that, wouldn't you?"

"I'm all in favor of cheap thrills."

Her cheeks began to crimson and I thought I was getting her back but then her eyes clouded up again.

"It just doesn't work for us," she said.

"I don't know what you're talking about."

"It simply doesn't. I know that I love you. I do know that, Eli. But it doesn't seem TO WANT TO WORK!"

My eyelids were getting heavy. Let this pass, I thought. Let this pass and we'll see about tomorrow.

"Maybe it's good," I said. "We're getting all this crap behind us."

"Perhaps. You're wonderful, Eli."

"How about a shower?"

That sensational Stephanie sigh. "Oh, Eli."

God how I loved this dame!

She kissed me and said goodbye and I went straight to bed. I lay there wondering what was to follow. Was this the final act, curtain, end of story? Where do you go when there's no place to go and what do you dream when there's nothing to dream? I realized, after about an hour, that I hadn't heard her car start. I looked out the window and her car was still there. I opened the door and there she was, still in the hallway, standing against the wall, arms crossed over her chest, shivering.

"Stephanie," I said.
She ran to me and hugged me. Then she left.

Chapter 15

The next night I went to visit Dad, as threatened, and the Reds were losing again. They had lost the night before, when all that had happened to Stephanie, but I refused to believe that when the Reds lose we all lose. As usual we didn't do much talking and in fact we didn't do any talking at all. I guess everything's been said or that anything he had to say he'd already said to Mom. He had the scorecard on his lap but wasn't keeping score as diligently as he used to. I could see it coming, as it had with Mom. One day you're surrounded by family, friends, neighbors, children, pets, by photos, mementos, trophies, and the next day you're in an empty room staring at the four walls of a nursing home.

I left after the sixth inning (he hardly noticed) and went out with Maishe to Maxy's in Mount Adams fiercely determined to get drunk. I told him about Stephanie. He shrugged as only Maishe could shrug. When it came to NOT CARING Maishe was the original. He suggested we try New York again, just get in the car as we used to, and just GO, except for the fact, I said, that we were getting old, surely OLDER, and it simply wasn't the same anymore. We were now MEN. That sounded strange to the ears, but we were. We were men.

Years before – when we were still GUYS – we'd jump in the car with Myron and a couple of others and agree to drive across the bridge to Covington, Kentucky, to pick up girls by shouting at them from the car, and not once, not one single time, did we ever pick up a girl that way, and yet, each Friday night we'd gather up and say, "Let's go to Covington and pick up some girls."

We were in our late teens or early 20s then, and though we had the regular crowd we lusted for those Kentucky girls.

"Strange pussy," was the motivation.

Maishe was onto his seventh beer. Maishe was incapable of getting drunk or even high. He could drink and drink and drink to no effect. I got drunk just watching him. He kept shaking his head. We sometimes spent hours like this, me drooling about this and that and Maishe shaking his head. He had no complaints, nothing specific, but he was upset that I had again turned down New York.

"You've lost it," he said.

"I haven't even found it," I said.

"You used to be ready for ANYTHING. You've gone stale."

We batted around names from our past, of GUYS who had metamorphosed into MEN and out of 15 came up with three lawyers, one accountant, three in computers, and all the rest in marketing. No comment necessary. Except for Maishe to note: "It's all marketing."

"It's all sales."

"Stephanie," he said. "Is that what's keeping you here?"

"Maybe."

"We're only wasting our time here," he said.

"Biding our time."

"Don't you know a person has to change his scenery once in a while? A change of place is a change of luck."

Now he laughed, about my degree in drama, and all the good it did in a place like Cincinnati, where BOWLERS, and even recreational ARCHERS, far outnumbered theater-goers. At least he had a degree in medicine, or something. Maishe was something of a chameleon. When we used to double-date he'd tell one girl he was a writer, another that he was an actor...artist, diplomat, international businessman, all of it true or false. Once in a while he was a general, or an admiral. The girls believed every word. Even if they didn't it still didn't matter because Maishe, more than anybody, had this way with women. Back in high school the girls swooned for him. Maishe took it all in stride. Once in a while he played into it as when the three of us had that accident on a county highway outside Lexington, Myron driving my car into a ditch. Nobody got hurt but when we came back to Cincinnati, Maishe had his arm in a sling and that drove the girls crazy.

Who but Maishe would have thought of that – certainly not Myron. Myron had no magic with women. Even the un-pretty ones thought they were too good for him. I once fixed him up and there he was in the back seat with her making out like Rudolph Valentino. She gave him practically everything she had. Next day I told her how glad I was that she'd hit it off so well with Myron and she said, "What? I couldn't stand that creep!" So like I always said, you just don't figure women. But creep that he was to the opposite sex, it was a given that in the end Myron, more likely than Maishe or me, would have the wife and the picket fence and the kids and the station wagon and the dog.

As for Maishe, the only sure thing about Maishe was that he was the most popular guy in high school, Woodward High, and later at UC. Even the teachers were smitten. He was so good at being young that he forgot what came next. So he simply refused to grow up and kept two apartments, one here in Mount Adams and the other on campus, right next to a sorority house, so he could continue to be adored. He wasn't getting older. He'd only submit that the girls were getting younger.

Maishe had money. Nobody knew where it came from. Nobody knew where HE came from.

Was he really Israeli? Where were his parents? WHO were his parents? Was his father really a general?

Maishe's proper residence was in the Rosemont section with his aunt. Was she really his aunt?

Even back in high school there were questions about his age. Some said he was in his twenties. Others said he was actually in his thirties. The girls wouldn't have cared either way, and nobody asked Maishe point blank about anything. At the outset, when he first came on the scene out of nowhere, maybe, maybe then a few questions were asked, but his responses were so vague that they satisfied everybody.

Chapter 16

When I got back to my apartment there was a note fastened to my door. Stephanie?

"Hey, Eli. Where were you? I hope you're not avoiding me. Eli, this thing between us, we have to get it settled. We can't go on this way. I can't stand it anymore. Too bad about her paintings. But it said so in the charts. I'd like to tell you about the rest that's going to happen. It's very important for you to know what's going to happen to her, Eli. The paintings were just the beginning. Love, Sonja."

* * *

As luck would have it, this was Friday night, which would leave me the entire weekend to brood and fret, except that it got worse in a hurry when the phone rang, Fat Jack, who seldom called me at home, especially at midnight, asking where I'd been all night, he'd been dialing me every 15 minutes – to tell me that he'd had a visitor in the showroom. (The bill collectors already had my cell phone number so I kept it mostly off.)

"A parole officer," he said, who'd been inquiring as to the whereabouts of one of his employees.

Took no genius to figure out who that was.

"She was in jail for seventeen months," Fat Jack said of Sonja Frick.

"What did she do?"

"Nothing much," Fat Jack said.

I was relieved. Shoplifting most probably.

"Except kill her father, that's all," Fat Jack added.

She had PREDICTED his death, as I recalled. Possibly, probably she had a way of helping her predictions along. ("They always blame me." From her own lips there at the start.) According to Fat Jack, she had been convicted of manslaughter after her father had been found knifed to death in his bed. Earlier, she had been found not guilty in the stabbing death of a boyfriend.

"Don't you check your girls out before you hire them?"

No I did not. I wasn't hiring Supreme Court Justices here.

"Girls generally don't commit murder," I said.

"Well this one did, at least twice."

"Well..."

"Well, Eli. Got yourself in a pickle, Eli. Told you to fire her."

I had also told myself not to hire her. I should have listened to myself first. Always go with instinct. That is handicapping for horses and for people.

"Now what do we do?" Fat Jack asked, in one of his rare vulnerable moments; actually seeking my advice.

We agreed we could not fire her now, not right away – unless we wanted the place burned down or something. She was a person to fear.

"She scares me to death," Fat Jack said. "You had to go hire a PSYCHIC? A nut? A lunatic? A murderer? Where's your sixth sense? Who knows what the hell she's up to. I only hope this doesn't get back to Harry Himself. We're done, if it does. We're sunk. Aren't there any more normal people out there, Eli?"

"Not at six fifty an hour."

"We're getting them from the bus depot now?"

"Certainly not from Vassar, Fat Jack."

"You're forgetting Stephanie."

"That was a fluke."

"Yeah, some fluke. I don't get it, Eli. You start off with a Stephanie and end up with a Sonja."

"True. Some people have all the luck."

"I hear she's got the evil eye for Stephanie."

"I'll worry about Stephanie."

"Wrong. I'll worry about Stephanie. She's my girl, too, you know."

In a way, she was. Yes she was.

"It's crazy what one person can do," Fat Jack said.

"Or undo."

"Open the door and who knows what the wind blows in."

* * *

I dialed Stephanie's number and her mother answered in that high society tone that smartly put you in your place. Her mother, not my biggest fan even when the sun was shining, and now it was raining, asked what business I had calling in the middle of the night, and I didn't dare tell her that, because of me, her daughter's life was in imminent danger. I just said it was urgent.

"Stephanie is out," she said impatiently, her usual tone with those of us who were not stakes-bred.

"Out?" I blurted. I hadn't meant to challenge the good woman, was talking mostly to myself.

"She doesn't always come home..."

Right here she was about to utter my name but either forgot it or decided that it would be too much.

Would be like admitting I was an actual person.

"Stephanie," she said, "has a mind of her own, you know."

I knew THAT, but I didn't know that other thing, that she didn't always come home. Really!

If she was out with a guy, that would be a worry. If she was out with a girl, that would be a bigger worry.

For that girl would probably be Sonja Frick.

Now THERE was something to brood about, which I did, considering the note Sonja had left on my door, a clear threat. In the morning I called again and there was no answer. In the afternoon I drove over and Stephanie's silver Jaguar was parked up the far edge of the circular drive – a glorious sight seeing that car!

Her mother, youngish in hair combed down near her shoulders, answered the door, didn't seem shocked to see me, the same way people weren't shocked to see pigeons. "Stephanie," she said, "is entertaining gentlemen callers."

Though she had grown up in Ohio, she was really a Southern Belle, her mother was.

Straight out of *Gone with the Wind*.

Gentlemen callers. All right.

"May I come in anyway?"

She opened the door wide, for uppity though she was, she was not about to be sullen.

Stephanie was in the den with them, the gentlemen callers, much laughter and happy nonsense filling the room, Stephanie rising to greet me warmly. She introduced me as "an old friend." The gentlemen callers she introduced by their first names AND their universities so that we had something like Joe Yale, Stephen Harvard, Rory Cambridge and even Lester Sorbonne.

"Join us," Stephanie said in a brand new society voice, sounding, in fact, a bit like her mother, which was to be expected as sooner or later she was bound to fill into the privileged role that had been assigned to her by birthright. What made Stephanie a winner was her ability to step in and OUT of that role, and her inclination to even poke fun at the part she had been genetically designed to play.

The gentlemen callers were scholarly and athletic, part of some university amateur wrestling team. A couple of them had their sights on the next Olympics.

One of them asked if I did any college wrestling and I said no, but Stephanie said, "Oh come on, Eli. Aren't you a black belt or something?" Okay, yes, I had a black belt in martial arts. They weren't buying this, the gentlemen callers, and one of them snuck up behind (as a test no doubt) and hooked me in a head-lock, and just as fast I dumped him and planted a foot into his Adam's apple.

This seemed a good time for them to leave, and they left.

"What a PERFORMANCE!" she said and fell into my arms laughing. "You were DIVINE."

Divine.

"Only doing my bit as AN OLD FRIEND."

"Oh, Eli," she sighed. "You took it all wrong."

She kissed me hard on the lips.

"You're so SERIOUS," she whispered, mussing my hair. Then: "Since you came back from New York."

"I thought I was funny."

"Even then you're SERIOUS, Eli. Oh so serious."

The rich are different from you and me. Oh – that's been used? Well they are, besides having more money. They recover. They move on. They don't sweat. Why just the other day she'd been distraught over her PAINTINGS and today? Today she was back to being Stephanie.

"Did something happen in New York?" she asked.

"NOTHING happened in New York. That's why I came back."

"I think something happened in New York."

"Nothing happened in New York."

"Some day you'll tell me."

I had questions, too, but wasn't about to ask where she'd been all night.

I had once asked her directly if she was a virgin, back when we spent that day at her country home, walking by the brook, not a question you generally ask a girl, but the moment seemed right, given the fact that she had asked me if any other woman meant anything to me, so I asked her and she blushed and said of course. Of course! That was before California, of course. I had not asked her since. I wouldn't dare, not only because this time she'd probably be offended but also because by this time she'd probably lost her virginity.

I now told her we had a genuine loony on our hands. I advised her never to go out alone, maybe hire bodyguards.

She thought that was even funnier than my earlier performance against her gentlemen callers.

"Oh, Eli," she sighed. "Do we have to be SERIOUS?"

"Bad things happen to rich people, too."

She laughed.

She said I was SWEET for worrying so about her. But she'd be fine. She patted my cheek.

"You don't understand what's going on," I said.

"Yes," she pouted playfully. "You're so much more MATURE than I am. YOU know what's going on."

"Yes I do and you're being a brat."

I was being MELODRAMATIC, she said, when I brought up the visit from the parole officer, Fat Jack's concern for her safety, Sonja's record of having at least two murders to her name, the note she had posted on my door about what's to come next. I was OVERREACTING because I felt such guilt at having brought this – this Sonja – upon our heads.

"You'll have to learn to say no to women," she said, softly and warmly and indulgently, meaning by that, I guessed, that one way or another, and sooner or later, a woman would be my downfall, given, as she had once put it, my ROMEO COMPLEX, one reason she could never take me really REALLY seriously, much as I tried to persuade her that, to me, she, Stephanie Eaton, was the beginning and the end of all women.

Now more than ever she was not taking me seriously, assuming, perhaps, that I was making all this up just to have access to her, which may have been partly true – the other part being that her life was in danger. That was also true.

"Go back to California," I said, meaning it, too.

She laughed. I couldn't get her off that rich girl high, that sense of hers that to be rich, young, and beautiful was to be impermeable. I was just like her mother, she said. I loved drama. "Oh," she teased. "Now you want me back in the arms of my WILD college professor? The one who puts lampshades on his head? Which he doesn't DO, by the way, but you were funny. You ARE funny."

Poking fun at him was a small victory but beside the point.

"Is this what you came here to tell me? To leave town?"

"Yes."

"Listen to you."

"Yes, listen to me."

"Why don't YOU be my bodyguard?"

I nodded, but my question was, for always or for tonight?

"At least for tonight," she answered without my posing the question.

So we had a date, our first since she'd been back. We went to a movie, then to Joe's Bar in Fountain Square, then for coffee and pie a la mode at Sugar n' Spice. She said she was just getting acclimated to Cincinnati again, after all those months in California, which wasn't nearly as fast as, say, New York, but was fast regardless, unlike Cincinnati, so it took some time to slow down, back to this town's tempo, and it really was a Midwestern town, Cincinnati.

"You don't really understand that," she said, "until you leave and come back. How Midwestern this town really is."

She looked down. She was thinking deep thoughts.

"But we always come back, don't we. You came back. I came back."

"For the time being."

"I'm not sure I like that," she said. She played with her spoon. "Are you thinking of leaving again?"

"Depends."

Long silence.

"On what?"

"Things."

"What things?"

"Things."

"Am I one of those THINGS?" she laughed.

"Maybe."

"Well, I'm not in such a hurry to leave again," she said. "I also have THINGS."

"Of course. You have family," I said, plainly fishing.

"Oh. But that wasn't what I meant. May I ask you a question?"

"If it's about WILD PhD college professors..."

"Oh, Eli. Be serious."

"I thought you don't want me to be SERIOUS."

"Well now I do."

I put on a serious face.

"Not THAT serious."

I slacked it a bit.

"Now you're clowning."

I changed my expression suitable for the occasion. It was one of the few acting jobs I could get.

"Eli," she sighed, "do you think that you'll love me always? Don't answer that too quickly. Suppose I turn old and gray? Suppose I age badly?"

"The way I feel now, yes, I'll love you always."

"That's the key phrase – the way you feel now. You might not always feel that way."

"Guess there's only one way to find out."

Was I proposing again? Was SHE proposing again? Would we always go round-and-round like this?

She smiled. "Aren't you afraid of the risk? You could wake up one morning next to a broken down old hag."

"You'd also be taking a risk."

"Looks don't mean so much to men. Looks mean everything to a woman, I don't care what they say."

"That worries you, your looks?"

"Sometimes. Sometimes I wonder if it's just the exterior men are after."

"There's the rest of it, too."

"I wonder."

"Stephanie, it's not the looks. It's the whole package."

"Package?" she laughed.

"You know what I mean. I mean I've dated many beautiful women, some more beautiful than you maybe..."

"EEEli!"

"Oh hell. What I meant was..."

She leaned over and kissed me softly. "I know what you meant. I can be very difficult, I know."

"Yes you can."

"I can be a real ballbuster."

"A real what?"

"You heard me."

"BALLBUSTER? That's not a Stephanie Eaton word."

"Are we about to fight?"

"It was not a Stephanie Eaton word B.C."

"B.C.?"

"Before California. Were you a BALLBUSTER in California?"

"No I wasn't. Eli...Oh, Eli."

"You came back a BALLBUSTER."

"You misinterpret. You misinterpret EVERY-THING."

"Stephanie Eaton. Ballbuster."

"Eli, I feel like smacking you."

"A smacking ballbuster."

She laughed happily. "YOU'RE the BALLBUSTER. Or whatever it is the other way."

"But I'd never use that word. I'm a gentleman."

"Oh sure. I'm sure you never use that word when you're with the GUYS."

"We never do."

"Oh I'm so sure."

"Right."

"Well I've heard guys talk..."

"Where? In California?"

She leaned back, straightened up and smiled.

"Let's drop the subject," she said.

Obviously California was going to be another sore between us. I hadn't intended it that way, I didn't know it bothered me that much, but whenever she came up with something new, something CALIFORNIA, it made me wonder, that's all. Made me wonder about this, that and a lot of other things. Never mind California. I knew what it was like when people left town, period.

"Maybe," she said tenderly, "we also need time to find OUR rhythm. The rhythm between us."

We finished off the night with some heavy breathing on her living room couch.

"Like old times," she whispered.

Chapter 17

When I drove to work on Monday I was still in that Stephanie glow – like living in a fairytale. Until...

Behold, there was a SALE!

The windows of Harry's Carpet City were plastered with signs proclaiming a 50 percent reduction on everything.

FABULOUS SAVINGS, the signs read.

Signs all over the place; the Second Coming could never be like this.

Fat Jack grabbed me by the lapels, shook me, and ordered me to change the telephone pitch to reflect the new gospel.

"But we're already saying FABULOUS savings," I said.

"Then say something else!" Fat Jack hollered.

"Like what?"

"You're the college graduate."

I pondered. "TERRIFIC savings?"

"EVERYBODY and his uncle uses TERRIFIC," Fat Jack sneered.

"Everybody uses FABULOUS," I sneered back.

"How about GIGANTIC savings?" Fat Jack offered.

"Why not MONUMENTAL?"

"Why not EXTRAORDINARY?" Fat Jack said.

"We've used them all," I said, "with about the same amount of luck."

"Oh yeah?"

"Oh yeah."

"Well find some new words, Eli. You're an ACTOR. Actors are supposed to know words."

"There are only so many superlatives in the English language, Fat Jack, and most of them have been used up."

"What did you say?"

"I said..."

"No, I mean superlative. Is that what you said?"

"I said..."

He smacked me across the head. I smacked him back.

"You're so dumb, Eli, you don't even know when you're smart. SUPERLATIVE. That's the word. For the new pitch."

"Brilliant."

"Speaking of dumb, what do you take me for, Eli? I'm talking about Old Lou. Where's he getting those million dollar leads?"

"What leads?"

"You know damn well what I'm talking about, Eli. Those QUALITY leads."

"Oh."

"Since when does a cripple like Lou Emmett close six thousand dollar sales? Not from YOUR leads. I'm not that stupid."

"He's getting them on his own."

"How?"

"Ask Lou."

"Fair enough. But be advised, his next wall-to-wall job could be his last."

"I know."

"In his physical condition he shouldn't be measuring a LOG CABIN, never mind those palaces in Kenwood. He's killing himself. He's half dead as it is."

"Goodbye."

"Yutz."

When I went upstairs Mona and the rest of the girls were busy dialing and Old Lou was waiting for me at my desk.

"I'll be rewriting the pitch," I said to Mona.

"Again?" she said.

"The new word is SUPERLATIVE."

She looked at me. "That's a big word."

"Aren't you tired of the old pitch?"

She shrugged. "Whatever works."

Just like Mona to protest, and then let go. Was that a Cincinnati thing? I often wondered, or was it something that came from being a wife and mother – or was it something that came with age? Was it a good thing or a bad thing, this tendency to retreat? Was it healthy compromise or defeatism? Maybe it was all that, or maybe it was just Mona.

Lou had a cigar tucked between his fingers. "Did you know I used to smoke cigars?"

"I heard you used to be one mean son of a bitch."

"I used to smoke cigars. Always lit one up after a sale."

"Been lighting them up lately?"

He chuckled. "Know what else I used to go for after a sale?"

"Let me guess."

"A lay."

"One good screw deserves another."

"I had more women than you could shake a stick at."

"I'll bet."

I was trying to change the copy on the pitch. Writing in SUPERLATIVE wasn't easy. Mona was right. Getting the girls to pronounce it would be the rough part. Only certain girls, for example, were meant for soliciting the better neighborhoods, like Hyde Park; those, let's say, who didn't come on with yiz or youz, or alls I know. Even the good ones, though, I couldn't get out of the habit of "axing" a question.

"I could go sometimes, five, six times a night."

I nodded.

"Did you hear me? Five, six times a night."

"I believe you, Lou."

"I had them knocking down my door."

"To get in or out?"

He flared. "What's that supposed to mean?"

"It's a joke, Lou. An old joke."

But Lou was steaming. "I had more women than YOU – and that's no joke."

"I thought I could joke with you, Lou. Thought we were pals."

"Not about women."

"Then about what?"

"Anything but women."

According to the story, Lou's wife had caused his heart attack. Also the stroke. Lou kept mum on the subject.

"Would you like it if I joked about Stephanie?"

"No I wouldn't, Lou," I said solemnly.

"So there you are."

Back in his day, he said, women were a challenge. Today they took their clothes off just for the asking.

There used to be virgins.

"A kiss was a big deal back then," he said. "Kissing wasn't what you call FOREPLAY. Kissing was IT."

"It's getting back to that," I said.

"Naw. There's no sincerity between men and women."

"What's the matter, Lou?"

"What do you mean what's the matter?"

"Something's eating you."

"Nothing's eating me. I'll tell you what's eating me. This guy. Out in Northwood. A new development. I got him from my QUALITY leads. I measured his house. Three floors. Plus basement." He started to cough, hacking. I thought this was the end of it right here for Lou. "I spent a whole day measuring. Now he wants me back. Says I measured wrong. I never measure wrong. Never."

"I think that's telling you something, Lou."

"That's telling me nothing."

"So you're going back?"

"Of course I'm going back. I do a job, I do it right."

"Who is this guy?"

"Out in Northwood."

"Who is the guy?"

"What's the difference?"

"I want to know who he is."

"Never mind."

"Want me to go with you?"

"What for? I'm a big boy." Then: "Sorry, Eli. It's been a bad day. Fat Jack." (Every place had a guy you could blame for everything. Just mention the name and everybody understood.) "Fat Jack's been on my back. He calls me a CRIPPLE in front of everybody, even in front of the customers downstairs. A joke's a joke, but enough's enough. He can be a real animal, Fat Jack."

"Believe it or not, Lou, he means well."

"They're the worst kind."

Chapter 18

Across the street at Ben's News and Smoke Shop, Ben was in a lousy mood and I had hoped he wouldn't be. I had a headache myself, probably from the heat, one reason I thought I'd get out of the boiler room for a while and visit Ben on the pretense of buying a Racing Form, though taking the afternoon off and going to the races was not such a bad idea if there was the money and the time. I needed a distraction, any distraction, but Ben had his own world to live in.

"They keep on coming."

A councilman, right here in river city, was proposing a ban on smoking in the sanctity of your home and automobile.

"What's next?"

This! A health food shop was "coming soon" up the street strictly for people, according to Ben, who cared everything about themselves and nothing for anybody else. Where's the no boozing frenzy to accompany the no smoking crusade sweeping the land, and who ever got run over by a smokin' driver as opposed to a drunken driver? The mobsters (that's what he called politicians and corporate CEOs) keep making new rules for everyone except themselves. We've all got a rap sheet. We're bar-coded from cradle to grave. There's a dossier on all of us. Orwell only got the date wrong.

Now it got personal. The racetrack turned down Ben's request for season's passes on the grounds that he had once been arrested for bookmaking. "That was 20 years ago," Ben said. "There hasn't been a book in this place since that time. They closed me down for a year. Chances are they'll close me down again, now that they've got me in their computers. You can't hide from their computers. But what's the difference. The wrecking crews are coming anyway."

"Here?"

"Haven't you heard? A new office building's going up. We're being torn down."

"No I hadn't heard."

"Well there it is. Everything comes to an end, right?"

* * *

Sonja failed to show up for work and never called in sick, not the first day, second day, third day... I was relieved. I was also troubled. Relieved that she was gone. Troubled that she really wasn't gone. Not this type. They don't just disappear. They come back. They always come back. I know this type. People like this shoot up kids in their classrooms.

But perhaps, I thought, she fell off a cliff. Even if she died, I wouldn't care. I'd care about the waste of a life. But not HER life. I was sick of LOONIES. When I was a kid the son of the people who lived downstairs was a loony, a schizophrenic who, of course, had his good days and his bad days, and always tipped you off when it would be a bad day, as when he'd bring in his own morning newspaper and not bring in ours. That was the signal. That meant whatever medications he was taking to regulate him weren't working, or he'd stopped taking them, and was liable to beat his mother and father. On such days he'd be waiting for Dad to leave for work, block his path and just glare at him. That left Mom alone upstairs and sometimes, in school, that's all I thought about, Mom home alone with this loony downstairs, and though I knew all about feeling sorry for the mentally ill, I couldn't help but despise this individual and whatever chemical, or hand, it was that that had created such a monster. Who NEEDS them? Who asked for them? Dad would call Mom every hour on the hour and warn her not to go down to the basement to do the wash. We lived in terror. We'd hear him bang his head against the walls. We'd hear the wailing of his elderly mother and father. They'd commit him – ambulances were on our street more often than the ice cream truck – only to have him sign himself out, as was allowed by the new, stupid law. I wished he'd go on banging his head. One day he banged and banged and banged, and then it stopped. The ambulance came. When they left with him his mother said he was dead. She said, "Now we'll have some peace." I didn't know if she was being realistic or sarcastic. Either way, I should have felt some remorse. But the only thing I felt was that it was OVER.

* * *

Sonja finally showed up, ho-hum, as if nothing were amiss, marched straight to her desk, studied the new SUPERLATIVE script, chuckled, and started dialing. She was back to being a blonde and this, dishwater tint, only illuminated the severity of her features. Mona looked at me, as did Marie, Denise and the others. I didn't know what to do, which was exactly what she told me when the rest of them broke for lunch. "You don't know what to do with me," she said. "Do you?"

"I thought you had left us for good."

"Wishful thinking?" she said with a trace of humor.

I asked her how she knew about the paintings, as mentioned in the note she had left on my door.

"You told me," she said.

So I had. I had actually told Mona, but loud enough for everybody to hear.

She answered the next question before I had a chance to ask.

"Those parole people have been making my life miserable," she said. "I was in jail for something I didn't do.

I shrugged.

"Do you believe me?"

I shrugged again.

"I DIDN'T DO IT!" she said.

"Okay."

Then, in a much softer tone, "You of all people should understand what happened."

Something was being said here – like what I did in New York?

But she couldn't know about that unless she were truly psychic, which I didn't believe. About anybody.

"Things happen," she said.

"Aha."

"You know how something can just HAPPEN!"

I spotted the bandage around her left wrist.

"Like that?" I said.

"I had an accident." Then: "Sorry about the note I left on your door."

"So am I."

"You have every right to be furious at me. That isn't really ME, this side you're seeing. I'm really not like this. No I'm not. I don't care what people say. They're wrong. You have no idea how much love I have to give, if only someone would give me half a chance." Tears were in order right about here but she didn't cry. "But it's not your fault. In fact I feel sorry for you."

"I think you've said enough. There's no need to get personal. This is only a JOB, Sonja!"

"You're right, and when I thought about it, how rotten I was to write you that note, is when I had the accident."

"You slit your wrist."

"It was an accident. I've done it before. Death isn't the worst thing, you know."

"It isn't?"

"There's something even worse."

"Like what?"

Now she smiled. She always smiled at the wrong places.

"Oh – things."

"Like what things?"

"Like finding out the truth. Do you forgive me?"

There really was no choice because once they started pulling the suicide routine on you – real or faked – the game was out of your hands. They OWNED you then. I'd had another one like that, years before, who committed suicide every Monday and Thursday. You knew they were using it, but you could never be sure.

"Please forgive me," she said. "I'll be a good girl. I didn't mean to complicate your life. You can see why I can't keep a boyfriend. I scare them all away."

"Bette Davis, right?"

"Please?"

I said nothing.

"I promise never to mention Stephanie again. I hope you both live happily ever after.

"Okay?"

I said okay.
"You won't regret this," she said.

Chapter 19

"I regret this," I said to Maishe that night over drinks at the Hilltop Bar in Mount Adams.

"Women," he said.

"People."

"Give us our daily temptation," he said, about a religious experience he'd had the other night; he'd been seduced by a preacher's wife. Maishe said he noticed something about us. We seldom had dates, regular dates with regular girls, and here we were, supposed to be the two greatest Romeos Cincinnati had ever seen – which was by itself a clue as to why we didn't have girls of our own. We usually had somebody else's.

That's why when holidays came around, even New Year's, we were usually home watching Dick Clark.

Or stuffing ourselves with chili dogs at White Castle next to a drunk singing My Melancholy Baby.

"Ironic," Maishe said.

"So the question is, why don't you have a woman of your own? Because the right one hasn't come along?"

"No.   Because the right one has, every other night."

Maishe had something going with Demona Karenina, yes, Demona Karenina, a Russian-Israeli lady who'd passed through our territory, from Los Angeles, to promote her new novel. She was a writer, of course, and gorgeous, and very much in love with Maishe and Maishe was in love with her, probably, but could not muster the enthusiasm to go chasing after her. Demona Karenina was roundly intellectual and hotly political and Maishe, if he wanted to, could match her smarts for smarts, politics for politics, but he didn't want to upon the proposition that, as to world events especially, it's all reruns. We're only repeating ourselves. He was tuned out and had dropped out some time ago when all that happened to him – whatever it was. Keep it simple and bring on the girls.

So it came to this – a preacher's wife. That hurt Maishe.

I asked him what denomination the preacher was. He didn't know. He said it wasn't the preacher he had in bed.

I asked him if he had ever made love to a rabbi's wife. He said yes.

"I've got to stop this," he said.

"It wasn't your fault," I said about the preacher's wife. Or maybe about the rabbi's wife, too.

"Of course it was my fault."

"You said she seduced you."

"But it still takes two."

"What denomination was the rabbi?"

"What do you mean?"

"Orthodox, conservative, reform?"

"What difference does it make, Eli?"

"Big difference. A reform rabbi, or even conservative wouldn't be so bad. But orthodox..."

"Eli, that was years ago, the rabbi's wife. The preacher's wife was last night. I've got to stop this."

"How did she seduce you?"

"She was visiting her daughter on campus. I was in the sorority house."

"You've got to start keeping away from those sorority houses, Maishe. Was she attractive?"

"I specialize in wives now."

"That's cause you're older."

"It's awful."

"So don't do it anymore. Quit. Like smoking."

"I think I will."

"Did she pray?"

"Eli..."

"I'll tell you why it's important to know her denomination. In case she has to confess."

"They don't mention names."

"How do you know?"

"She told me. She said she wouldn't use my name."

"She told you she was going to confess."

"I'M confessing, aren't I? To you."

"But I don't give forgiveness or salvation."

"We've got to stop this, Eli."

"We?"

"You're no better."

"I've been behaving."

"No more wives. That's my slogan."

"I really can't feel sorry for you, Maishe. If I felt sorry for anybody it would be the preacher."

"Thanks."

"I've never had a preacher's wife."

"But you had a politician's wife."

"That's no sin."

"Yes it is, Eli."

"But not as unholy."

"Something's wrong with us," Maishe said.

"That's a fact."

Chapter 20

Sonja showed up at my apartment the following night and I wasn't surprised. They really do keep on coming.

She swore there'd be no repeat of the other night when she had run out after me naked and screaming. The reason for this visit was orgasm, which she had never experienced, most likely, therefore, the root of all her problems. Like her split bi-polar personality. Her restiveness. Her jealousies. Her frustrations. An orgasm. That was all she wanted from me. Then she'd leave me alone.

Why me? I wasn't in the orgasm business.

She said, "Girls talk, you know. You're something of a legend."

"Talk is talk. I'm really not that good."

"I'll take my chances."

Before I could stop her she was naked and under the covers and here I had thought we had played this scene before.

"Join me?" she cooed.

I lit a cigarette.

"Most guys light up after," she said.

145

Her first joke.

"Thinking about it?" she said. "Go ahead. I've got all the time in the world."

I was sure she did.

I figured if I got up and left she'd only follow me, naked and screaming, and I was in no mood for that again – or, I could comply, get it over with, which I'd never do for a thousand reasons, mainly that that's not what sex was for, that's not what women were for, and it certainly wasn't my destiny, either, to provide orgasms unto the Miss Lonelyhearts of the world.

"Can we put some music on? I notice you like classical music. That goes on for HOURS."

Not quite what Beethoven had in mind.

I turned on the TV, sat down, watched and listened to the laugh-track howling at every sitcom word, and it occurred to me that this canned laughter may have been recorded 30, 40 years ago and that what we were listening to was the laughter of people who were DEAD. After a couple of these sitcoms she said, "Is that all?"

I handed her the remote control.

"Don't you want to find out more about me?"

I knew all about her, plenty.

"I've completed the course."

"You're no actor. You're nothing but a boiler room operator."

"I could have told you that all along."

"I'll bet you're lousy in bed."

"I've been telling you that all along."

She started to get up and get dressed. "You call this hole your APARTMENT?"

"Actually I call it a hole."

"I can't imagine why anybody would want to live in Mount Adams. It's all yuppies. I'll bet all your friends are yuppies."

"I have no friends."

"Why I ever wanted you, I'll never know."

"Same here."

"You and that rich bitch deserve each other."

Now she was drilling near the nerve.

"That hot shit bitch. You probably think she's a virgin."

Now she was on the nerve.

"I wish you could see her as I see her. Maybe some day you will."

With that she slammed the door.

Chapter 21

We were on the Ohio River on Covington Landing, a floating bar and restaurant. There was a full moon and the stars were bright.

We were both a bit tight from a couple of Manhattans.

"Don't you wish we were alone now?" Stephanie said.

We were among a thousand other celebrants from both sides of the river. We were sitting at the bar.

The Covington Landing was the IN place.

The OHIO RIVER was the IN place.

After her third drink she started dancing with some guy, which I didn't mind, since I bragged about the fact that I couldn't dance.

White men can't dance.

So then a scuffle broke out when this guy she was dancing with wouldn't let go. He wanted her for keeps. This wasn't much of a scene, but enough. I rushed over and calmed the guy down. He grew calm when I held him by the scruff with one hand and with the other hand applied pressure to the bridge of his nose. I said everything was all right.

He said, "Pardon me."

I walked her back to our seats and asked if she wanted to leave.

"No," she said. "I won't let some idiot ruin a perfectly good evening."

She said things like this always happened when we were together. "What is it with us?"

She shook her head in exaggerated disbelief.

I said, "It's not us. Funny things seem to happen when you get tipsy."

She admitted I had a point. "I lose control when I drink."

"It loosens you up?"

"Too much."

Did it loosen her up in California? I didn't ask. We'd only go round again.

"You have to see to it that I don't drink anymore."

"I can't be with you all the time."

We were now outside admiring the stars. A cool breeze was coming up and she gripped my hand.

"That's too bad," she said.

Was she hinting? Was it time for me to propose again?

"Are we falling in love again?" she asked.

"I've got nothing better to do."

She said she had a serious question. "Why do you stay at Harry's Carpet City?"

"It's a job."

"Have you tried? Have you been looking?"

"Not really."

"Why not?"

I shrugged.

"Something happened in New York. Didn't it, Eli?"

"Why do you keep saying that?"

"Fat Jack once suggested that something very traumatic happened to you."

Here I thought Fat Jack was my friend. But he was Stephanie's friend, too.

"How did he suggest?"

"Well you know we always talk. I asked him why he thought you limit yourself so."

"What did he say?"

"He said he was sworn to secrecy." She gave a nervous chuckle. "Do you have a record or something?"

The fact was, I didn't know, still. They had released me with such speed that I didn't have a chance to ask if I had anything on my record.

"You know what I wish?" she said.

"What?"

"I wish we could start all over."

"But we are."

"Are we?"

"Are you ashamed that I work at Harry's Carpet City?"

"Not really. But I just don't want to see you stuck, that's all."

"You want me to be like your GENTLEMEN CALLERS?"

She laughed. "You know I don't. I just think every person should try to fulfill himself. Are you fulfilled?"

"Is anybody?"

"But you're not even trying."

"You can't be sure."

"Do you still dream of becoming an actor?"

"Yes, I still dream."

"But dreaming won't do it, will it, Eli?"

"You sound like a girl who's been talking with her mother."

"I sound like a girl who's getting serious about a guy."

"You sound like a girl who's had a couple of drinks."

"I don't need liquor to turn me on to you. Have you stopped believing in me?"

"But life goes on, remember?"

"You're not going to hold that against me."

"I've just learned to be cautious."

"There's cautious and then there's dead. Have I hurt you that much? You've hurt me, too. You'll never know how much. We only know how much WE'VE been hurt. We're experts at that. We never know how much we've hurt the other person. Put that in your pipe."

"Didn't you once tell me all you wanted was freedom?"

"You once said the very same thing. I've had my freedom."

"We talking about California?"

"In a way."

"You...experimented."

"In a way."

"I see."

"Not THAT way, Eli. Not everything is SEX, Eli. But I got to know people. I told you when I left that when I came back I'd love you more, or I'd love you less. That's the chance you take. Well, I found out that even in California, people are just people, and then there's you, Eli."

"I'm special."

"You're not letting me be romantic, Eli. What's the matter?"

I didn't know what was the matter.

"Is there someone else?" she asked.

"Don't be ridiculous."

"So why all this static?"

"Maybe I love you too much, Stephanie. Maybe I'm unfit for you. Maybe I'll never get to be an actor. Maybe I'll always be stuck at Harry's Carpet City. Maybe something did happen in New York. Maybe none of it, some of it, or all of it, Stephanie. I don't know. I swear, I just don't know."

"We seem to take turns blowing chances."

"But I do love you."

"Eli, I love you, too. I love you very, very much. So what's our problem?"

"Maybe that's our problem."

Chapter 22

Lou was coming up the steps and Mona and I locked eyes; it was taking him longer and longer to make the trek. You could hear him starting and stopping. You could hear him breathing. I had hired a couple of new girls in the meantime, girls who had never seen Lou and knew nothing about him, and they were frightened, wondering what it was that was approaching.

"It's only one of our salesmen," Mona whispered to the fledglings.

Now the long pause at the top landing so he could make a decent entrance.

"Hello everybody. Hello Mona."

His hairpiece was askew. He was sweating. His face was yellow.

"Hi, Lou," Mona said.

He plopped down and took a few minutes to catch his breath.

"I see you got yourself some new girls," he said. "That's good. Could use some fresh blood."

"You all right?"

"Never been better." He leaned over. "I see you got rid of what's-her-name, that Sonja."

"No I didn't. She just hasn't shown up."

Not since the latest scene in my apartment. Which gave me the willies wondering what she was up to. I wanted her around just to keep an eye on her. She hadn't been around for days. I tried calling her but the numbers she gave on her application form were out of service. She had given a place in Price Hill as her address and once or twice I thought about taking a ride over there, imagining her dead in the bathtub, water and blood spilling over onto the tiles. I imagined her tracking Stephanie, lurking in the alleys. For all those reasons I wanted her here and even considered giving her that orgasm, if that would do the trick and keep her from doing harm.

"What's wrong with YOU?" Lou asked.

"Me?"

"You're as nervous as a jellybean."

He asked if it was about what's-her-name Sonja.

"Is she your problem?"

I shook my head.

"She seems to give everybody fits," he said. "Is she jealous of Stephanie?"

"What makes you say that?"

"Just guessing. I know Stephanie is back."

"You measured that house again?"

He coughed and said yes he had.

"Is that all?"

No it wasn't. The developer was so pleased with Lou that he was giving him the carpet business for an entire unit of homes out there in Northwood.

"Twenty-two homes," said Lou. "What do you say about that?"

"I say that's a hell of a lot of measuring for one man."

"I told you those leads were GOLDEN."

"I told you they were stolen."

"Guess who's going to make the Million Dollar Club this year?"

"Hope you're around to collect the medal."

"You worry too much," he coughed, and coughed and coughed and coughed.

"You all right, Lou?"

"You always act as if I'm going to die any minute. I'm not that old, you know. I'm only in my fifties."

ONLY IN HIS FIFTIES? I could have sworn he was well up in his seventies.

Phil Coleman, the man they called Hot Shot, charter member of the Million Dollar Club, walked up just in time to hear that last one and said, "Sure, Old Lou here is still a young man. He's one of our stars. You know, those stars that keep shining for years and years after they've gone out."

He checked around the room for admiration, smile as wide as the devil's. It was an amazing thing for Phil Coleman to come up here, for Hot Shot that he was, he didn't need my leads. He didn't want my leads. Considered them "the bottom of the barrel." He got his leads direct from downstairs, off people who had phoned in or just come in to browse. Browse my eye. Soon as they meandered in they were hooked once he got his fangs into them. Customers just casually entering the showroom for "a hallway rug" didn't know there were seven HUNGRY salesmen in there waiting to pounce on them. That included Morris Silver, except that Morris didn't sell anymore. He just sat there at the big table telling stories.

"Why is it always JOKES with you guys?" Lou said, which was strange, coming from Old Lou, who was always fearful of the big three since he was a much lesser salesman from the time of his stroke, inferior in terms of sales and stature – but not so since he got his hands on those QUALITY leads and was now in business with an entire housing DEVELOPMENT.

"Jokes?" said Phil Coleman. "Nobody takes you more seriously than me, Lou."

"You're always cracking jokes."

"Calm down, Lou."

"I'll calm down once you get out of here."

"Oh? Eli's your man?"

"What's the trouble, Phil?" I piped in.

"No trouble. No trouble at all. I just wanted to know if you got any leads. For the rest of us."

"Why now?"

"I hear this is the place. For hot leads and hot chicks."

He looked around and gave me a wink.

"I don't know about hot chicks..."

"Word gets around."

"I don't know about hot leads, either."

"That's not what I hear. I hear Lou's scoring big. Where you getting those leads, Lou?"

"What's it to you, Phil?" said Lou.

"I want in on the action."

"We just got lucky," I said.

"That's some job out in Northwood. Some luck, twenty-two homes."

"But I keep giving you leads, Phil. I spread them around."

"Not like the ones you've been giving to Old Lou here, lately."

"You worried I'm going to have a better year than you?" said Lou.

"Hey, I'm on your side, Lou. I'm one of your fans." He winked at Mona, who didn't wink back. She was wise to him. He was full of winks and grins, this Phil Coleman. "Don't forget, I've thrown a few leads your way," Hot Shot Phil said to Lou. "How soon they forget, right Lou?"

"Yes, I remember that kitchen linoleum job."

"Hey, can I help it if it didn't pan out? All I can do is give you a lead. It's your job to sell."

"I'm TEN TIMES THE SALESMAN you are."

Lou was going for his second stroke.

"Hey, Lou, you're the greatest," Phil said for his exit line.

Lou chuckled. "He thinks that Northwood lead came from you. It's killing them down there that I'm back."

He said, "You hear me? Lou Emmett is BACK."

157

Chapter 23

Sonja finally showed up, emaciated. She'd been sick. An accident. Too many sleeping pills. Three days in intensive care.

"I'm too hard on myself," she confided with a show of weariness.

"Not to mention everybody else."

"Why should I always be the one who suffers?"

"Guess what? You're not."

"I've done a lot of thinking," she said, "and I know what's at the bottom of all of this."

"What's that?"

I was curious.

"It's a certain individual."

I shot her a look.

"Oh not you," she said. "Someone else."

"Who?"

"You'll find out," she said smugly.

Then she ran to her desk.

I walked over and told her she was fired.

"I'm not surprised," she said.

Then, out in the hallway, she said: "But you should have done it sooner."

Then: "You should have never hired me, you know."

Then: "Do you really think there are such things as casual relationships? You think what's between us is casual, so casual you can get rid of it by just firing me? Do you really think once I'm out of here I'm gone? Goodbye? So long? Guess again. Haven't you ever heard of DESTINY?"

Then: "Oh, God! If you only knew what was coming. You poor thing. Goodbye."

When I walked back into the boiler room I was greeted by applause.

"Good riddance," said Denise. Marie hadn't said a word to me for weeks, from the time she'd made that weekly arrangement with Fat Jack and thought that I had set her up, or maybe I just thought so. But now she said: "Finally!" Mona congratulated me. She said I had done a smart thing. I wasn't so sure.

* * *

I went to visit Dad and we both sat in the living room of his apartment in Avondale listening to the ballgame on the radio. Keeping score as he was (was he in remission?), and depleted from illness as he was, he hardly knew I was there, and of course I wasn't offended. In fact I was comforted in that at least this much hadn't changed; there was still baseball, and still Dad listening to it on the radio, keeping score as if his life depended on it (and maybe it did), puffing away at his old briar pipe.

He wasn't always an old man. You tend to forget that about old people.

I remembered his taking me to my first ballgame, up in the bleachers, when some burly son of a bitch accosted him about his pipe (which wasn't lit), saying, just as we were sitting down, "Hey stupid, you're not going to keep puffing that pipe in my face all game long, are you, stupid?"

Dad ignored him.

He still hadn't lit up and never would, in public.

"You start puffing that pipe and I'll shove it up your ass, stupid."

Dad ignored him.

The guy got up to leave after the seventh inning.

Dad nudged me and said, "Time to go."

Which surprised me. Dad would never leave until the last batter was out. Turned out we were following the guy down the steps, outside, into the parking lot and even into his car, which was where Dad grabbed him by the neck and began choking him until and guy turned red, white, and blue. Dad kept whispering, "Never ridicule a man in front of his son."

Now Dad said, "Nothing's as bad as it seems."

Was he talking about the game? The Reds were winning.

"So long as you're alive," he said, "nothing's final."

Chapter 24

I was in my apartment when Stephanie called. She said, "You know how you're always making fun of me for being so rich? You said if the cook ever went on strike Mother couldn't find her way to the kitchen. Well guess what? The cook took the day off and Mother didn't know where the pantry was. I swear."

She was laughing.

"I'm sorry we had such a rotten time the other night."

"Oh, Eli. You were just being Eli. I forgive you. There'll be other nights."

"How about tonight?"

"I can't. I've got to run. Bye."

She hung up.

I called back.

"You have a date?"

"Not exactly."

"But you're seeing somebody."

"No I'm not seeing anybody. I'm going out. All right, I'm seeing that girl you fired."

"SONJA?"

"There, I knew it," she said.

"SONJA?"

"I knew I shouldn't have told you."

"SONJA?"

"I don't want to argue about this, Eli."

"How did this happen?"

"She called. She wants her job back and she wants me to talk to you."

"That's not it at all. She wants to kill you, Stephanie."

She laughed. "Eli, you're being dramatic again."

"Stephanie, this girl is dangerous. There really ARE people like that, and I don't mean WILD."

"You can't stop me. You're being foolish. We're only going out for coffee, for gosh sakes. Girl talk."

"Where?"

"I don't know. I love you. Goodbye."

* * *

I PEELED RUBBER to catch her before she left. If no cop spotted you, Cincinnati was a fine place to speed because, here, even the pedestrians waited for the light to turn green before crossing, no matter how late the night, how remote the neighborhood – people froze at the corner and waited for the light to change, first because the police gave tickets for jay-walking, and second, the German influence. You did as ordered. You behaved. You were a Cincinnatian.

Stephanie's car was in the drive.

Her mother answered the door, as always offering absolutely no expression, a remarkable feat of acting. You couldn't even call her STONEFACED because even stones have expressions. Look closely. I knew it was an act because I knew how lively she could get when the RIGHT people were around. More than lively.

GUSHY! I had even seen her and her husband drunk once, and what a show that had been, so embarrassing that Stephanie felt compelled to apologize every day for a month, me saying it was forgotten, which it was, because if I were to remember it, that scene where her mother came into the den slobbering and teetering like that and asking if I knew any dirty jokes – if I were to remember that I'd have to reconstruct my entire image of the Eaton family, all of Hyde Park and all of High Society included, and I wasn't in the mood to undertake such a thing.

"Stephanie is out, Eli."

"Oh."

"She just left."

"Do you know where?"

"No I don't."

A symptom of rich homes. Nobody knew where anybody was. Rich homes were like corporations.

I was glad she wasn't asking if there was anything wrong, but she might have asked SOMETHING, to establish some sort of – rapport? Was I really mashed potatoes in her eyes? Stephanie, laughing that high laugh, had once told me her mother thought me CHARMING. She also considered me a PHASE her daughter was going through.

"Thank you," I said.

"Yes," she said.

I lingered by the door. To her it must have been loitering.

"I'd invite you in," she said, "but I'm cutting roses."

She was cutting roses.

I walked back to the car, drove off searching for her, her and that fruitcake Sonja. Why was Stephanie wasting her time with such a lowlife? It made sense because Stephanie, despite her highfalutin ways, considered nothing and nobody beneath her. I drove to the address Sonja had given on her application. Price Hill. A man in his early thirties, quite tall and very thin, came to the door. He said he was related to Sonja Frick all right. He was her brother.

"Sometimes I'm her husband," he said with a smile. Most of his teeth were missing. He spoke Kentucky drawl.

She didn't live here anymore. "Gone back home...I guess."

Home was Covington.

Did he know where she was this minute?

"You from that parole board?"

I told him who I was. He told me who he was. Wayne. He laughed. "Yeah, she's told me all about you."

"Do you know where she is right now?"

"Nobody knows where she is right now," he joked. "Know what I mean?"

Did he know if she was out with Stephanie?

"I heard her mention the name. No love lost there, right?"

"Right."

"She's really got it in for the girl. You know Sonja. She can get mean. Did she do something to her?"

"That's what I'm trying to stop."

"Well you better git on your horse, Mister. Sonja's all business."

He gave me the address in Covington, but he wasn't sure if she was still in the same house.

I asked him about Sonja's clairvoyance.

"Yeah, she sees the future all right, and if it don't fit, she makes it fit. You know about Dad."

"Did she..."

"What's your guess?"

"I don't know. What's yours?"

"She hated Dad. Dad had a bad AURA, she said. She said the same thing about that girl..."

"Stephanie."

"Said she had a bad aura. She sees auras, you know. I don't think she meant to kill Dad. Just his aura. If it means anything to you, that's probably what she has in mind for this..."

"Stephanie."

"She just wants to break her aura."

I felt like a stand-up comedian. Everything I said cracked him up. He couldn't stop laughing.

I said, "Do you consider your sister..."

"Sometimes my wife..."

He said it – Maw Wauf.
"...dangerous?"
"Fuckin' A."

Chapter 25

Only a few years following her COMING OUT party, first in Cincinnati, then in New York, then in Palm Beach, at which the rich and famous from all over the universe came to pay homage – old money knew no boundaries – only a few years after that Stephanie Eaton came to work for me at Harry's Carpet City as a PHONE SOLICITOR.

Go figure.

The ad was in the paper and she responded. She'd had a fight with her parents, one of many, and to prove she was INDEPENDENT, to hell with Daddy's millions, she was going to get a JOB. Not a debutante job. But a job. A job job. She called and from the voice alone I knew I'd hooked a rare one. She asked me where we were located. I wanted to say Fifth Avenue, New York. Or Rodeo Drive, Los Angeles.

"Vine Street," I said.

I thought I heard her gag.

"Do you have any other locations?" she asked politely.

"You mean like Paris, London, Rome..."

She laughed and it was a good, honest happy laugh. "My only concern is that you're too far from me."

"Where do you live?"

I knew she'd say Hyde Park.

"Hyde Park," she said.

She heard me laugh and said, "Did I say something funny?"

"No, I'm just wondering whether you've called the right place. This is HARRY'S CARPET CITY."

"I know."

"Are you aware what we pay an hour?"

"It says in your ad."

"And you still want to apply?"

"I'll be there tomorrow morning."

"Are you sure?"

"I'll BE THERE," she said with uppity resolve.

"This isn't the Riviera."

She laughed. "See you at nine. On VINE Street."

But nine o'clock came and she didn't. Usually I didn't bother when they stood me up like this, they were, after all, a dime a dozen, but this was different. I knew because sometimes you just know. So I found Eaton in the phone book, on Rosebush Lane – where else?

"Did you forget?"

"Oh God, yes. I did. That's POSITIVELY unforgivable. I'll be right over."

"You must not need a job very badly."

"Oh yes I do. Please. I'll be right over."

"You remember where we're located."

"Yes. Vine Street not the Riviera. Give me an hour."

I gave her three, before she pulled up in that silver Jaguar.

Fat Jack had taken notice. As she made her way up the steps, he called up to ask. "Are we hiring royalty? That car's worth more than you'd make in ten years, fifty years, a hundred years – and look what's walking up into your lousy boiler room! Will you look at this! Eli, this girl's a DREAM. Marry her."

"I'd like to meet her first."

"I give you two weeks."

She arrived wearing a frilly, billowy top and tight skirt, which didn't go together, in fact didn't go at all, and I figured she had dressed for the occasion – for Vine Street. She had too much rouge on. Hardly any lipstick. On the thin side, but great breasts, which were being held in reserve. Beautiful? Oh yes. But I didn't fall for her the minute I laid eyes on her. Took a good five minutes.

I had expected her to be cool and classy, which she certainly was, but you could tell that she was a socialite in the making, not quite finished yet, something too gangly about her still, a bit unsure of herself, lacking absolute refinement and complete poise, which would come, you knew it would come, any day in fact, any minute.

She sat there appraising me and I wondered which one of me she was seeing – the company man or the artistic rebel. One minute a knowing smile would sweep across her face as though letting me know that the big desk wasn't fooling her, but the next minute, as I was explaining things, she'd nod reverentially.

I gave her an empty desk to fill out her application but instead of writing she kept shooting me worried glances.

"This isn't a test," I said.

I'd never seen anyone tackle a lousy application form with such sincerity and intensity, even fear.

"Ready whenever you are," I said, but that would never happen, it was plain to tell.

She'd never be ready.

"Whatever you've got will be enough," I coaxed.

Finally she got up and just stood by my desk imploringly. I reached out to take the paper from her hand but she wasn't letting go of it; as many times as I reached out she pulled back. She finally handed me a sheet that was empty save for her name, address and education. Vassar.

Fat Jack leaped into the room, grabbed the paper, crumpled it up and said, "Forget this. You're hired."

Then he vanished.

She laughed.

"That was Fat Jack," I said.

"I know. I met him downstairs."

"He thinks I ought to hire you, no questions asked."

"Oh? He told me we ought to get MARRIED, no questions asked."

We both laughed.

"I notice that you've never held a job before."

She shrugged and began smoothing the boxing trophy that was on my desk. She blushed when I said she didn't have experience.

"Are you aware that people down here can be awfully crude?" I said, thinking of Fat Jack in particular.

"Am I hired?" she said impatiently.

She had switched gears on me.

Of course she was hired. But I still had to do the interview!

I said the only skill required in this job was the ability to read a script into a telephone 100 times a day, and perhaps be persuasive, that wouldn't hurt; come up with one or two leads a day. That was the easy part. The hard part was the atmosphere of a boiler room, not to mention Vine Street, which was really not the sort of boulevard she was used to, if I judged her correctly.

"I'm not THAT sheltered," she said, seemingly amused by my paternal attitude.

I said muggings were not uncommon on the street.

"I'm a big girl."

I said she'd be wise to have her chauffeur drive her over.

She laughed. "What makes you think I have a chauffeur?"

"Everything about you."

She blushed.

"Most people hang up on you," I explained about the job. "Everyone you talk to is a stranger."

171

"I'm sure I can handle it," she said playfully but decisively.

She wasn't taking me seriously and continued toying with my boxing trophy. That was the only thing there was of me around the office and she did comment about it, about how I obviously wasn't much for décor. There were no photos here of me or of my family, no trinkets, no mementos, other than that boxing trophy. She said that people who don't nest in obviously intend to move on.

"Your job is to get leads," I said.

"You told me."

"Do you know what a lead is?"

"I guess it's an appointment you try to set up for a salesman."

"Absolutely. You know much more about this business than I thought."

She thought I was joking.

"What does your father do?" I asked.

She shrugged. "Daddy? I don't know. Well I do know. But I really don't know."

"I just wondered if you knew anything about sales. Because that's what this is."

"No I don't."

"You've had pests calling you on the phone to buy this or that, and you've probably hung up on them."

"Probably."

"Well that's what you'd be doing. You'd be one of those pests."

"Good."

"As you know, you're vastly, ridiculously over-qualified for this job...for any job."

"I don't care."

"You are a debutante, aren't you?"

"Oh there was some silly party."

"So I'm not far off. Why do you need a job anyway?"

"That's personal. Oh all right. Mother was being IMPOSSIBLE, as usual. Or more than usual."

She said that as if I knew MOTHER. Doesn't everybody know MOTHER?

"Since Fat Jack walked away with your application form there are certain questions I must ask for the record."

She turned very serious for these important questions.

"Are you married?"

"No."

"Do you have children?"

"NO!"

"Are you engaged?"

"No," she said, catching on.

"Are you going steady?"

"This is for the record," she said.

"Official business. It's for the FBI. Clearance."

"No I'm NOT going steady."

"Are you in love with anybody?"

She blushed but quickly recovered. "This is for the FBI."

"No, the CIA."

"You can tell the CIA I'm not in love with anybody. Am I CLEARED?" She was still playing with my boxing trophy.

"Can you start tomorrow?" I said. "Or do you have to go shopping first?"

She sighed and gave me an exaggerated brush-off. "No I don't HAVE TO GO SHOPPING. I'll be here tomorrow."

For the first week we kept our distance, playing it formal; the second week we started talking books; the third week she confessed to being an artist; the fourth week I confided that somewhere deep inside I was an actor; the fifth week she started to skip lunch with me; the sixth week she began staying late; the seventh week she asked me to box with her. Then we wrestled. Then we kissed. Then she started coming over to my apartment and sighed a lot.

She made up with her parents, which meant she didn't need Harry's Carpet City anymore.

She could BUY Harry's Carpet City, as Fat Jack kept reminding me.

But she stayed. I asked her why.

"Guess," she said.

The other girls took to her. She played no uppity games with them.

Mona loved her.

Fat Jack came up regularly, dragged us out into the hall, and said: "When are you two kids going to quit fooling around? Get married." To Stephanie: "You love him, don't you?"

"You're embarrassing her," I said.

"No he's not," Stephanie said. "Yes I do love him."

"So what's your problem?" he said to me.

Downstairs Fat Jack grabbed me by the tie. "Don't let this one get away, you YUTZ!"

But I did.

Maybe I did.

Chapter 26

Fat Jack was telling the salesmen that if business didn't pick up in a hurry there'd be no Christmas bonuses this year and there might not even be a Christmas PARTY. "Him and his CHRISTMAS PARTIES," whispered Morris Silver. "We haven't had a Christmas party here in ten years. TWENTY years. We NEVER had a Christmas party."

"So what are you complaining about?" said Phil Coleman.

"Christmas party," said Morris Silver.

Fat Jack was saying, "Harry Himself is thinking of coming down to talk to you men. And you know what that means!"

That means the earth will shake. There will be thunder and lightning. Trees will topple. Rivers and oceans will run backwards. Dogs will meow. Cats will bark. The birds will grow silent. Mountains will roar. Harry – like God – wasn't seen anymore. Nobody saw him arrive. Nobody saw him leave. But we all knew he was here, UPSTAIRS, listening, watching, privy to everything, even our innermost thoughts. He was Harry Himself. There was none like him. Not on Vine Street. Not in Cincinnati and not in all of America. Harry Himself could sell any-body anything. He didn't have to anymore. He was worth, according to Fat Jack's estimate, maybe twenty million dollars – and still HUNGRY.

Make that THIRTY MILLION and still HUNGRY.

He had started the business selling REMNANTS door-to-door, operating from the back seat of a broken down Chevy. He got the remnants from GARBAGE cans, the scraps left over in the alleys by the department stores like Shillito's and Pogue's. Now, of course, he was a leading philanthropist. He was married and had one daughter, adopted, a girl named Sasha, now 24, who had married a wimp accountant, Stanley, a bean counter who would eventually take over the business, a sickening thought to Fat Jack. Stanley wasn't a salesman. Accountants were inheriting the earth.

I had once been to Harry's office. He sat behind a tiny, tidy desk that had nothing not even a computer or a pencil on it, and there he sat so un-ferocious, so tame, so TIMID, so untrue to his legend. The office had obviously been designed by a woman for a woman and, in fact, his daughter Sasha was an interior decorator. The only thing he had going for himself here was an ashtray and a box full of cigars. One reason he stayed late was that his wife wouldn't let him smoke those things at home. He asked me a few questions about how things were going, and thanked me for my time. He never mentioned the boiler room, which led me to believe he didn't know what I did around here, or that he even had a boiler room. He thanked me several times. He seemed very tired, in a way to suggest that he had seen everything and nothing could ever surprise him, and there were even hints of disgust at the corners of his mouth to mean that people had disappointed him, that it wasn't all roses at the top and that if he had to do it over again maybe he wouldn't. He thanked me again. He was a NICE GUY. Which was a very disillusioning thing to know. You wanted him to be GREAT and POWERFUL and AWFUL. It took months of not seeing him and Fat Jack's repeated invocations of the Harry legend to gradually build back the awe and terror in me.

"We got a man here," Fat Jack now continued to the assembled sales force, "who can barely WALK. He's a CRIPPLE. And what's he doing? He's putting all the rest of you men to SHAME! He's closing wall-to-wall jobs left and right. That's right. I'm talking about Lou Emmett. That old cripple over there, that has-been, is going to make this year's MILLION DOLLAR CLUB! Before anybody else! That's right. Lou Emmett. He may be a cripple, but he's ten times the salesman you men will ever be!"

Later, upstairs, I said to Lou, "Well, what do you think of that? He made you feel like a million dollars."

"By calling me a cripple?"

"Lou, why is it always the negative with you?"

"He called me a cripple. In front of everybody."

"He also said you were ten times the salesman they'd ever be."

The wear and tear of being so great a salesman was beginning to show on Lou. His contract with that guy over in Northwood called for him to measure a house a day; close to 25 homes in all.

"Why one a day?" I asked.

"He's in a hurry."

"Lou, you're shaking."

"Something happened. Promise you won't tell anybody."

"What happened?"

"Promise."

"What happened?"

"I'm driving back from Northwood yesterday. I was very tired, Eli. I'd been measuring this house all day and I was very tired. I'm driving back. I'm someplace in Walnut Hills. A kid, this kid runs out in the middle of the street. Right in front of my car. I nearly ran him over. It was THIS close. I almost forgot to put on the brakes I was so tired. That really shook me up, Eli. I've had nightmares all night. I keep seeing myself slamming on the brakes, and nothing happens."

"But you did slam on the brakes on time."

"But I ALMOST didn't. You'll never know how close it was! What if it happens again?"

"You don't even have a license."

"You better not tell anyone about this."

"Lou, forget this Northwood deal. This guy's asking too much. Who IS this guy?"

"He's the developer."

"WHO'S the developer?"

"It really shook me up. All night I dreamed about hurting this kid. Running him over."

"This can't go on, Lou."

"You know what scares me? Maybe I did run the kid over."

"What are you talking about?"

"Maybe I did. Hasn't that ever happened to you? You hit a bump on the road and you wonder?"

"Did you go back?"

"Yes. I didn't see anything."

"So there," I said.

"But imagine, thinking you may have killed somebody. Can you imagine?"

Yes I could imagine.

"How can a man live with himself?"

He puts it out of his mind. Every minute of every day.

"Don't you dare tell Fat Jack I was tired."

"I promise."

"That's all I'd need. He'd pull me off. I'd be finished. Are we pals?"

"We're pals."

* * *

Fat Jack said I looked awful. "No I mean really awful," he said. "Terrible."

We were down in the stockroom where miles of carpet were rolled up against the walls, arrayed like beautiful dead animals being skewered, a perfect spot to do some boxing. Fat Jack loved to spar. One time I opened a cut over his left eye and he bled all over a WHITE rug. We both laughed our heads off after we buried that bit of evidence that was worth around $18,000. Now he came to me and said, "You can't TOUCH me." Touch him? He was so open I could have floored him by just saying boo. But I never would, of course.

"You're not so tough," he said after we traded harmless jabs for a few minutes, him doing all that dancing and prancing as if he were a prizefighter with the championship of the world on the line. Then he switched to wrestling, pulling me down in a headlock. Then he grabbed my tie and twisted it, saying, "I want to know what's going on. So tell me."

So I told him. I told him Stephanie hadn't been home for three days and three nights, ever since she'd met with Sonja. I was worried, worried sick that Sonja had harmed her. I called her home. Her mother had assured me that Stephanie was fine, staying at some friend's house – but would tell me no more.

"So what's the problem?"

"I don't think she's with a friend."

"You think she's been kidnapped?"

"I don't know."

"That fucking Sonja."

"I never should have hired her. I never should have fired her."

People like that, you don't know what to do. Whatever you did was wrong.

Fat Jack comforted me by saying, "That's what you get for being such a cockmaster..."

"I never went near her."

"...going from one broad to another. One of them's bound to be a lemon."

"I know it's all my fault."

"Yes it is all your fault," he said, offering further comfort.

"If anything's happened to Stephanie..."

"There's nothing you can do, Eli. Her own mother says she's all right."

"Her own mother hates my guts. She lies."

"There's nothing you can do, Eli, except wait. Stephanie'll call. She always does."

Chapter 27

But she didn't. Days turned into weeks. Always, it seemed, since the time I first met Stephanie, the purpose of my life was waiting in general and waiting for the phone to ring in particular, and now when it did ring and it wasn't her, I turned nasty to whoever it was, especially if I was at home and some pre-programmed phone solicitor was trying to sell me magazines or tickets to the policeman's ball or something – until I remembered that's what I did for a living. MACHINES, in some cases, were now doing the soliciting, which didn't bode well for my future in the business. I was in the wrong business anyway but still no phone call from New York, if ever. Give my regards to Broadway.

Man dreams, God laughs, but it's not funny.

Marie, Fat Jack's Monday afternoon delight on false pretenses, ended the boycott against me and said, "I'm not seeing him anymore."

I pretended like I didn't know who what where when why.

I gave her a dumb look.

"You know, don't you?"

I shrugged.

"You don't?"

Another dumb look. If I pull this off, I AM an actor.

"Of course you know."

"Know what?"

"About me and...oh, you know. I know you know."

"It doesn't matter."

"I know it doesn't matter. To you. Nothing matters to you."

"That's not true."

"Someday I'll tell you why I did it," she said.

"All right."

"You don't know women at all. If you did you wouldn't have hired that witch."

"You're right there, Marie."

"Some of the girls, we've been talking, and we decided we never seen you so miserable."

"Thank you."

"That ain't no compliment. Where's Stephanie?"

"I don't know, Marie."

"Mona thinks Stephanie...Stephanie's hurt someplace."

"Mona?"

"She's worried. We're all worried."

"That includes me."

"What are we going to do about it?" Marie asked.

Now there, I thought, is character.

"You're something," I said.

"What do you mean?"

"I mean you're okay."

"We're all ready to help."

"If I think of something..."

"Just say the word, Eli."

I thought of something. I pulled Mona out into the hallway. I told her I had searched for Sonja in Covington at that address her brother Wayne gave me, and there was no such place. But I was convinced she was somewhere in Covington, probably with Stephanie. We had that Internet Criss-Cross section devoted to Covington, which we never called, because it was low-rent. But now might be a good time to solicit Covington, not for carpet but for Sonja. We'd use the familiar pitch for selling carpet, but just to get a response, to hear a voice. Sonja's voice had a sharp twang to it, a slight shrill that was unmistakable when she got to talking, so that it would be important to get the people talking, at least saying a few words, before the usual hang-ups. Fortunately, for the new girls, we still had Sonja's audition tape – thanks to the automation introduced by Fat Jack when he thought it might be wise to test the girls on tape before hiring them.

"I know this will cut into your leads," Mona...but just an hour a day. All the girls."

"Of course. I'm as anxious as you are."

"Fat Jack mustn't know about this."

"I know."

We had thousands of names to cut into and it was slow-going at an hour a day, so I upped it to two hours, then three – until finally it consumed all eight hours of the working day. Through my extension I could listen in on any conversation, which I did whenever I got the hand signal that someone was HOT, and so many sounded almost like Sonja, but almost wasn't enough.

The enthusiasm in the boiler room was something to behold. Now the girls had a purpose. They were driven. On their own, they cut their lunchtime in half, cut out their breaks altogether, and suddenly there wasn't all this going to the bathroom. They tore into the work with abandon and hit the high points of the script, which went something like this:

"Hello."

Pause for response.

"How are you today, Mrs. Blank?"

Pause for response. First rule of salesmanship – get the other person to respond.

"Isn't this weather... wonderful... awful... (depending)."

Second rule of salesmanship – get the other person in the habit of responding in the affirmative.

"My name is Mona Waters (depending). I'm calling from Harry's Carpet City. Have you heard about our sale?"

Usually the answer is no. A desired response.

"Well good, Mrs. Blank. This gives me an opportunity to tell you about our superlative savings on all our brand names. Of course that includes Bigelow, Karastan, Salem, Galaxy, Burlington Stain Resistant Plush, and even the finest Oriental makes, like Beaulieu of Belgium."

At this point the person says she's not interested. But the solicitor doesn't hear this.

A good solicitor hears no discouraging words. She ploughs on. "Well Mrs. Blank, our field specialist (read: salesman, but a word that must never, ever be used) will be in your neighborhood all week (which wasn't true) and he'd be glad to stop by..."

Really, I'm not interested.

"Will you be home tomorrow, Mrs. Blank?"

I said I wasn't interested.

"Say around three, Mrs. Blank?"

I said I WASN'T INTERESTED.

"Mrs. Blank, this sale only lasts one week."

I don't care.

Now the good phone solicitor, having got this far, uses every weapon available.

"You're under no obligation."

I really have to go now. I have a crying baby.

"Can you afford to pass up these savings? Don't you owe it to your family?"

I'll worry about my family. Now I'm going to hang up.

"Only a few minutes is all we ask. So can I put you down for three o'clock tomorrow?"

"Let me just check your address..."

I'm hanging up.

As a last resort: "Look, my job is on the line. Please give me a break."

* * *

Fat Jack didn't know what was going on except that he was getting more leads than ever for his men, a happy development until it turned out that most of them were for LINOLEUM. Fat Jack ran up, looked around and asked me to join him downstairs.

"Something's funny," he said. "There's trouble in Carpet City."

"What?"

"Something's wrong."

"What are you talking about?"

"The girls. They're so enthusiastic!"

"That's bad?"

"Half hour lunches, no coffee breaks – no going to the john every five minutes."

"This is a complaint?"

"No, but Covington is. Covington? Since when do we solicit Covington? They're all hillbillies."

"I thought we'd give it a try."

"Yeah, and you're doing very well – with LINOLEUM! Hillbilly carpet. LINOLEUM."

"All right..."

"All right hell. You've got some of my best salesmen wasting valuable time on LINOLEUM."

"Well, now we know about Covington."

"We always knew about Covington! What's going on, Eli?"

"Going on?"

"You think I'm STUPID?"

"No I don't think you're STUPID."

"I'm not STUPID, Eli."

"I never said you were STUPID."

"You think Harry Himself would have made me manager if he thought I was STUPID?"

"No, Harry Himself wouldn't do that," I said.

"You think HARRY is STUPID?"

"No, Harry's not STUPID."

"So what's going on? I have a right to know. I pay the bills."

So I told him.

I told him why we were calling Covington.

He said this was a BUSINESS. This wasn't a place for detective work. If I wanted to find Stephanie I should go to the police. I could get fired for this. Get all the girls fired, too, including Mona, who'd been here since CREATION. I was ruining people's livelihoods, including mine and his. Harry Himself would have his head for this, if Harry ever found out. Harry would go through the ROOF. Using salaried employees for your own personal benefit was a disgrace, even unethical, even if the intent were honorable, as in saving a life. Saving a life was one thing, but this was DOLLARS and CENTS we were talking, which was bigger than life and death.

"Everything you say is true, Fat Jack. You're correct on all counts."

He wasn't poking me in the chest or twisting my tie. He was truly upset.

"You know I can't let you do this," he said.

"I know."

"It isn't fair to the COMPANY, you understand."

"I understand."

He stared at me. I stared at him.

"But if I know you, Eli, you are going to DEFY me."

"I think so."

"Of course," he said. "You're in charge upstairs. I don't HAVE to know what's going on. Catch my drift?"

"Aha."

"I mean if you keep calling Covington, I don't have to know that, so long as nobody tells me."

"Who's to tell?"

He grabbed me by the shoulders. He whispered, "One week. I give you one week."

* * *

Mona said Lou had called while I was downstairs. He sounded very bad.

"Wanted to talk to you in a hurry," she said. "He'll be calling back any minute."

Had he finally run somebody over? Without a license?

"He was out of breath."

"But he's always out of breath."

"Not like this, Eli."

She shook her head.

I shook my head.

She sighed.

I sighed.

"Lou, Lou, Lou," I said.

"I know what you mean," Mona said.

I waited for his phone call. Finally it came. This was the story: He was out in that Northwood development, some 20 miles from Harry's Carpet City, and he couldn't move. He had been measuring this new house. The first floor went okay, but then, walking up the steps, he had collapsed. He crawled back down and made it to the phone.

"I'm dizzy," he said. "Can you come get me? I'm afraid to drive."

Was it another stroke? I asked. Another heart attack?

"Dizzy," he said. "Very dizzy. Please come get me."

"Can you give me directions?"

He tried, but he was all mixed up.

I said I'd call an ambulance.

"Please don't. I'll be finished. Fat Jack'll never let me go out again. You know he won't. Don't do this to me, pal. Just pick me up, is all I ask. I'll be all right. I just need to rest. Are we pals?"

He did manage to give me the address.

"Please hurry."

I ran down two steps at a time. Fat Jack was busy with a customer, which was good.

I dashed to the parking lot where my car was and as I was about to put my key into the ignition a hand hit my shoulder.

"Where's the fire?"

I tried to lie but Fat Jack knew all the lies. He was a salesman. So I told the truth.

He slipped in on the shotgun side.

"Let's go," he said.

Good thing, too, that he was coming along, because I really had no idea where this place was, me and my terrible sense of direction, which had earned me the nickname Magellan.

191

"You'd have been heading SOUTH without me," Fat Jack said.

"I know where I'm going."

He took that philosophically. "Where the hell ARE we going, Eli? Here's a guy who may be dead by now on account of a CARPET sale." I'd never heard Fat Jack disparage carpet. You never knocked the product. "Here I am," he continued in a reflective vein, "married, and I was paying a hundred bucks a week for a piece of strange pussy. Where the hell am I going? Where the hell are YOU going, Eli?"

"I don't want to talk about it, Fat Jack."

"You're a boiler room flunky! That's all you are! Ever think about it in those terms? You're not an ACTOR. You're not on BROADWAY. You're on VINE STREET. You're not married to Stephanie Eaton. You don't even know where she is! You'll end up marrying on of those two-bit Covington broads. Worse, NEWPORT! You'll have a house-full of LINOLEUM! You'll go BOWLING Saturday nights. That's where you're going. You had your chance. You're a fucking failure."

"Are you a success, Fat Jack?"

"Yeah I'm a success. I'm manager of Harry's Carpet City. I make one hundred and eighty thousand dollars a year, plus commission. I got a house in the suburbs. My wife golfs in the CLUB. My kids go to private school. I have a gardener."

"And you've been paying for strange pussy."

"Well – YOU tell me what that means?"

"It means you're a bigger loser than I am."

"You're probably right, Eli. You're probably right."

"Harry Monocle," I said. "He's a success."

"Oh yeah? He stays late in his office upstairs, sometimes till midnight. You want to know why? Because he hates going home. He hates his wife. His wife hates him. Their daughter hates them both. He hasn't talked to Sasha in five years. SIX years. He despises his wimp son-in-law. For all his millions, Harry DOESN'T EVEN HAVE A HOME!"

It wasn't often that we talked like this.

"Harry's whole life has been carpet," Fat Jack said, "and making money, and look where it's got him! Where's HE going? I don't think he's got a friend in the world. Carpet, carpet, carpet. Sell, sell, sell. So our wives can walk around in mink coats – and then you die. Like Old Lou, that poor son of a bitch. What the hell does HE live for?"

"Carpet, carpet, carpet. Sell, sell, sell."

"I think, between you and me, he wanted to kill himself. That's what I think, Eli."

"He ain't dead yet."

"He knew he was driving himself into the ground. Measuring a house a day. In HIS condition. Now you tell me!"

"I think somebody was trying to kill him."

"I wouldn't be surprised. How did he get hold of that Quality list anyway?"

"How did you know he had it?" I asked.

"Eli – I know EVERYTHING. Everything."

"He wouldn't tell me."

"Well, we'll find out. That's who killed him."

"Why do you keep saying he's dead?"

"My instincts say he is. Did you know he was once our top salesman?"

"So you've told me."

"You know what we used to call him? Iron Man. He could go out on seven calls a day. He was one mean HUNGRY son of a bitch. Did you know he had a wife? A son? He'll never talk about them and no one knows what happened. Man works his balls off all his life to come to THIS?"

Which was exactly what the preacher said, if not in so many words. Only a few salesmen attended the funeral service. Morris Silver was there; the Big Three couldn't make it, they were out on calls. Mona was there and so was Harry Himself, and that would have made Lou proud. Fat Jack was there, of course.

The preacher said that we should not think of Lou Emmett as he had been the last few years. Forget THIS man, he said, pointing to the casket. Try to remember THAT man, the earlier, the younger, the vibrant Lou Emmett. Forget the man who had been broken by illness. Think back...

Later, outside, I asked the preacher what he was talking about. "I don't mean to be disrespectful, but Lou HAD been vibrant. Even if not, I still want to remember Lou as he was in the end. There was NOTHING WRONG with him. A heart attack and a stroke crippled him? So what? Did that make him less of a man than you or me? What was wrong with him in the end that would make you say we should forget him?"

"You misunderstand me."

"There was nothing wrong with Lou."

"You misunderstand me."

"You insulted him."

"You misunderstand me."

Fat Jack stepped in and pried me away.

As we drove back to Harry's Carpet City, Fat Jack said, "You misunderstood this guy."

"He didn't even know Lou. Lou never went to church. He never got close to a preacher, unless it was to measure his living room. He had no right talking about Lou the way he did. I kept worrying he'd call him by some other name. The guy probably does a funeral a week. You think he really knows who's in the box? You think he really cares? To the rest of us it's a funeral. To him, you know what it is? It's another SALE!"

Fat Jack cracked up laughing. He was close to tears.

Maybe he wasn't laughing.

Chapter 28

I paid a visit to Stone Kiley of Seats Galore, the recliner king, the guy who had developed the Quality list Lou had borrowed or found or stolen. Stone Kiley reminded me of a pool sharp, slicked back hair, mustache, raspy voice, wise-guy slouch, not at all your basic Cincinnatian – and that name, Stone Kiley, and that death-hold handshake, and that room-full of hunting trophies, and that hustler friendliness. Some guy.

He offered me a tour of his boiler room but I declined. I knew what a boiler room looked like. He said he had 30 girls working for him pitching everything from recliners to insurance to siding. He was very proud of his operation. He had a very fancy office. His air conditioning worked. I asked him if he knew about Lou.

Yes he did and he was so sorry. "Lou used to be the best."

He asked how Mona was. He knew Mona. Her mother-in-law worked for him.

"Some day I'll steal her from you," he joked about Mona.

"Did Lou steal those leads from you?" I caught him off guard.

"What's the difference?" He shrugged. "Lou's dead."

I suggested murder.

"Oh?" He chuckled. "And who made you a cop?"

"Just nosy," I said.

"Man ought to watch where he sticks his nose. Hey, I'm a busy man. What do you want?"

"I notice you're on the board of directors of Northwood Development Corporation."

"You NOTICE? How do you NOTICE?"

It was really quite simple. Even after Lou's funeral I couldn't bury him, in my mind. I knew he had been murdered...this business of giving him all those houses to measure...what was that? Maybe not in the strictest sense of the word, and maybe not in the eyes of the law, but it was murder. One phone call clinched it; routine request to the public relations office of Northwood Development Corporation for its annual report on the pretense that I was interested in buying a house and wanted to know more about the company. I knew I'd find the name there, and there it was all right, Stone Kiley.

"You have evidence?" he said.

"You were going to get even with Lou for stealing that list from you so you fixed it that he got that Northwood deal. You had a cripple on your hands. A stroke victim. So you were going to work him to death...give him all those homes to measure...ONE A DAY."

"That's evidence? I never touched the guy."

"No, you had the manager of Northwood, that guy Cliff Roberts, make him the deal. But it was YOU."

"Maybe it was. I was doing Lou a FAVOR. Maybe I LIKED Lou. I told you I liked Lou. So I was gonna do him a favor. Gave him all the business. A salesman's DREAM. You gonna have the cops arrest me for giving a salesman TOO MUCH business? Tell that to a judge! Tell it to a jury!"

"But we both know that you killed him."

"Suppose you're right? Sue me. Take me to court. Now get the fuck out of here."

He got up. I got up.

I clenched my fists.

"You can't touch me," he said.

"Maybe I can take you to court..."

"I said you can't touch me – and you know what I'm talking about."

No I didn't, unless he knew about that other thing. Logically that was impossible. But you had to account for this mysterious business of people knowing things about you that they weren't supposed to know. There were no secrets.

"Now get the fuck out of here before I call the cops."

I counted my choices and came up with zero.

Chapter 29

When I got back to the boiler room Mona said she had a lead on Sonja. Mona had called this number and the woman on the other end began to laugh and then finished the spiel, even using the word SUPERLATIVE. Then she hung up. Mona couldn't say for sure that it was Sonja's voice because, truth be told, she said, she and the other girls had lost their sense of voice-detection, as drink and food tasters eventually lose their sense of taste from over-indulgence.

I dialed the number and the voice said: "Very clever, Eli."

"Sonja?"

"Have you been looking for me?"

"I've been looking for Stephanie."

"I know. Wayne told me."

"Where is she?"

"How would I know, Eli. You fired me, remember?"

"Weren't you with her?"

"Yes I was. We had a long talk. She's some girl, Eli. Too bad."

"What's too bad?"

"Oh you don't know. Stephanie had an accident."

I gulped without saliva.

"Did you hurt her?"

"I can't hear you, Eli. You'll have to speak up. Have you lost your voice?"

"Did you hurt her?"

"Nobody hurts anybody. Everything's preordained. How many times have I told you that? It's destiny."

"Where is she?"

"You don't know?"

"I don't know."

"She's home. She's been home. I think you should see her, Eli – the real Stephanie."

* * *

I called Stephanie's house. The same story. Her mother assured me that Stephanie was staying at a friend's.

I didn't believe her, of course.

"I'd like to talk to you," I said.

"We're talking," her mother said.

"I'd like to come over."

"That won't be necessary."

"I know Stephanie is there, Mrs. Eaton.

She hung up.

Chapter 30

That night Maishe phoned from a sorority house.
"Let's talk," he said.
"Can it wait?"
"We have to talk."
"Tomorrow?"
"Meet you in half an hour."
We arranged to meet at Maxy's.   There was a
strange urgency in his voice, over the phone, strange
for Maishe, who was never urgent about anything,
never even had a phone for that reason. He'd argue
that nobody ever really needed a telephone, nothing
was ever really that important, except maybe once in
a lifetime. This sounded like that once-in-a-lifetime.

As I walked over to Maxy's a half hour later I realized that this was the first time I dreaded seeing
Maishe. He obviously had information. The streets
of Mount Adams were quiet and it was an impossibly
hot, muggy day. So much had changed over the past
few years, ever since the PCs, the Politically Correct
moved in and took over and mowed the lawns and
manicured the dogs, their neat BMW's parked in
front of the slopes. I also wore tennis shoes but mine

were REALLY torn. You live in a place too long and soon YOU become the stranger.

I walked very slowly because nobody is in a hurry to hear unpleasant news. As long as you don't know a person is dead, that person is still alive.

I needed to keep Stephanie alive.

"Have a drink," said Maishe.

"I don't want a drink."

"Have a drink."

I ordered a screwdriver. Maishe was losing his hair, I noticed more and more. Maishe was aging. I looked at Maishe, I saw myself. He still had his looks, but time was running out. One thing was sure gone, that cockiness. Even that casualness was getting a bit studied. Was he getting stocky? I didn't know. You see a person so often you can't tell the changes so readily. But he seemed to be getting husky.

He asked me if I believed that bit of wisdom which insists that everything is for the best.

Even the greatest tragedy.

I was quick with that one. I said a real sign of maturity was when you no longer believed everything was for the best.

"Then I have very bad news for you," he said.

Wrinkles on his brow. Crows feet under his eyes.

"Stephanie is dead," I said.

"No," he said. He lit a cigarette but without the usual flair. He used to have a way with a cigarette.

"Then what can be so bad – and how come you know things that I don't?"

"Stephanie's mother called me."

"Why you and not me?"

"Let me finish. She didn't want to talk to you because..."

"Because she hates my guts."

"LET ME FINISH, for fuck's sake." Maishe never swore. That was one of his charms. "Because she knows you're in love with Stephanie and I'm just a friend. So she confided in me, as a friend. All right?"

"Confided what?"

"Eli, you're not going to take this well. I know you."

"Try me."

"Stephanie's been disfigured."

I nodded. I felt nothing. I felt stiff and hard and cold.

Disfigured. What did that mean? What the hell did that mean?

"Did you hear me?"

I nodded. I heard the roar of a motorcycle outside. Made me wince. I hated noise. Too much noise in this world lately. What are we trying to drown out?

"Did you hear me?"

"Disfigured. Yeah. I heard you."

"Snap out of it, Eli. You have to take this."

"How bad?"

"Eli..."

"How bad?"

"Give me a CHANCE, Eli! You think I like this? I've been living with it for days. I had to tell you today because her mother said she couldn't put you off any longer. So that's why it had to be today. But I've known about it..."

"How bad?"

"Permanent."

"There's surgery," I said.

"Yeah, that'll help some, and you know she'll get the best treatment. But she won't be the same. Not even close."

I knew better. I knew there was surgery. They did miracles these days.

Rich people like the Eatons can BUY miracles.

"You're taking it well, Eli. Or are you taking it too well? I can't tell with you."

"I'm fine. Sonja, of course. Right?"

"Yup."

"What happens to Sonja?"

"You want revenge?"

"Aha."

"Right now Sonja's not your worry. Stephanie's been trying to take her own life."

"I refuse to believe that," I said.

"Her whole face. Her whole body. She was knifed up and down."

"Have you seen her?"

"No. This is all from her mother."

"How long until I can see her?"

Maishe shot me a startled look. He asked if I'd been listening to him.

"Never."

"Who's to stop me?"

"You'll never get in that house."

"SOMEDAY Stephanie's got to step out."

He shrugged. "I'm not sure. Look, Stephanie's a dream. Keep her that way."

"You know I'll get to see her, one way or another."

"Then you'll be destroying her dream, too, about you. This may be small comfort at a time like this, but you're the last person Stephanie wants to see. Because she's in love with you. That's what her mother told me. You'll never see her again, Eli. Get that through your head. There is no more Stephanie."

Chapter 31

We were having a Going Out of Business Sale. Fat Jack proudly announced it to me when I walked in, after I saw the signs outside – Everything Must Go. I was surprised. I had thought business was good, even though business was always bad. Fat Jack was in a terrific mood.

"We're closing shop?"

"What makes you say that?"

I pointed to the signs.

"Oh that! That's our latest advertising campaign."

"You mean we're not going out of business?"

"Why should we go out of business?"

"My mistake."

This was like the time we had a fire sale, except that there had been no fire. When the Ohio River flooded we always had a Flood Sale. The Ohio River was miles away. Harry Himself had gained GENIUS status within the retail community when we had tried to trademark the word SALE, so that nobody else in America and perhaps the world could use the word without breaking the law, or paying him royalties, and even though the attempt failed, the legend continued.

I told Fat Jack I wouldn't use that pitch upstairs as it would be unethical and he gave no static.

But he added: "You're no salesman."

"Thank you."

He wanted the latest on Stephanie.

I said she was in California.

"So you lost her again," he said and I said yes, I lost her again.

The best way to forget about her, he suggested, was to hire a bunch of new girls.

"Fresh blood," he said. "Fresh pussy."

That wasn't such a bad idea all of a sudden.

I interviewed a beautiful blonde named Donna Mylstrom, from Clifton Heights – incredibly beautiful. Put movie stars to shame. Her resume said she had finished high school and had one year of college. I had never heard of the college, but she was going back after she saved some money to train for something paralegal, or para something. She had a body that refused to quit. I gave her the voice test, which she flunked. She had no voice. She whispered and had absolutely no oomph. She'd never get a lead.

I hired her.

First day on the job she walked over to my desk all flustered. She was hemorrhaging. She was so embarrassed. She protested when I offered to drive her to the hospital. On the way there, to the Jewish Hospital, she said the bleeding had probably stopped, so I drove her home. "I'm so embarrassed," she said when I dropped her off. "You don't know what it's like to be a woman," she said.

"No I don't," I said.

"I'll make it up to you," she said.

A week later I had her over to my apartment in Mount Adams and she was terrific in bed, although I kept worrying about a repeat of her problems. You really didn't want them bleeding all over your lily white dick unless you were going to marry them and even then it wasn't much fun and only proved what Maishe had always said, that women were more than just tits and ass, unfortunately; they bled, they had headaches, they got into moods. That's why you went from one to another. Soon as one started to bleed, you moved on. Anyway, Donna Mylstrom had taken care of her problem just in time and was really terrific, really sensational, really superlative in bed. She didn't do much. She just spread her legs, which was quite enough. She was so gorgeous. I loved her nipples. She was so gorgeous that I thought this could be a lasting thing – weeks! She came over every night and it developed into something of a routine. We walked in, threw our clothes off and went right to work. No lights out. No music. No talk. I just drove straight into her and worked her until she screamed.

Then I drove her home. I had no complaints. She did.

"You never talk," she said.

I shrugged.

"You never talk to me," she said.

"Is something wrong?"

"No."

I was giving her my body. What more was there to give? She was so beautiful.

I tried talking to her but every topic was a topic I had already covered with Stephanie. I told Donna that it might be best if she found a guy who talked. I didn't do talk. Talking was extra. She said it was all right the way it was. I didn't have to talk but I persuaded her I wasn't right for her, so she quit the job and was gone.

Every night after work I drove over to Stephanie's house in Hyde Park and parked down the bottom of her drive. I knew where her room was and thought of climbing up. I stayed parked down there for about an hour, then drove off. I drove there this night and a cop was there in the drive. He asked me what business I had. Checked my driver's license. Told me to leave and never come back. I was back the next night and the cop was still there, so I left.

I hired a few more girls, four of them. Two of them were named Sue. I took them both to bed, at different times. One was married, the other had a boyfriend. I learned that these things didn't matter. The other two were named Carol and Barbara and I took them to bed, too. They all complained that I didn't talk. Barbara, or maybe it was Carol, complained that I didn't kiss.

"All we do is go straight to bed," complained Carol, or Barbara. Or maybe it was Sue.

Marie, Fat Jack's old standby, was next. She offered to cook me dinner. She cried while I drove her to my apartment. She cried while she cooked us dinner. She cried while we ate. She cried while we made love. She cried after we made love. I put on the ballgame and watched the game.

She asked why I didn't wonder why she was crying. Wasn't I going to ask?

"In a minute."

The Reds had runners on first and third.

When they failed to score I said, "Why have you been crying?"

She explained that she had become Fat Jack's mistress only to please me.

"That doesn't say much for me," I said. "I'd never ask a woman to do something like that."

"I was afraid I'd lose my job. I support my mother, you know."

"I'd never fire you over something like that."

"Maybe not you. But what about Fat Jack?"

"He'd never EVER do that, either."

"You don't know men," she said.

"You don't know Fat Jack," I said.

She cried.

She said I had forgotten what lovemaking was for, that I made love like other people drank or took drugs.

For the diversion.

I hired two girls named Kathy and I liked one better than the other, Kathy Ann Sanger was the one I liked, and I decided to love her. I decided to TALK to her and take her places. But I couldn't take her to

Fountain Square. All of downtown Cincinnati belonged to Stephanie. The ball park was out, since I had twice taken Stephanie to ballgames. Kathy Ann wanted to go to the Covington Landing on the river, but that was out, of course, since that also belonged to Stephanie. Forget Sugar n' Spice. Forget Joe's Bar or Maxy's.

So we ended up in my apartment every night and even the walls laughed when she said: "You never talk. We never go anywhere."

* * *

Maishe said, "Let's go to New York."

I shrugged.

"There's nothing here anymore, Eli. Cincinnati's finished for you."

"There's Sonja. I'm not finished with her."

"You want revenge?"

"Justice."

"What world do YOU live in?"

Even Stephanie, Maishe explained, wasn't seeking justice. She wasn't pressing charges.

"Of course not," I said. "She'd have to appear in court and obviously, after what was done to her..."

"She doesn't want to appear anywhere," Maishe agreed.

211

Chapter 32

The summer was coming to an end but it kept getting hotter. Even September wouldn't let go. Ben, over at Ben's News and Smoke Shop, said it was the ozone. Soon it would be summer all year round. He asked me if I had read Philip Wylie, who had explained it all, and also, by the way, had explained all about Momism, the philosophy that blamed all the world's troubles on over-protective mothers. That made Ben laugh. Only Mencken made sense, and a good cigar. He was retiring anyway, so it didn't matter that in a couple of months or weeks the wrecking crews were coming. He was only worried about Hank, his partner, who was in the hospital with a heart attack, maybe over losing the business, maybe not; he had a bad heart.

"A shame," Ben said about Lou Emmett. "He had started buying cigars again."

Ben had been packing up, ready for them to come move him out. He had much valuable stuff here. Souvenirs, mementos that went back to World War Two. Once upon a time this had been the hub, the crossroads.

"Wait a minute," he said.

He went to the back and returned with a baseball, and a well-worn baseball it was.

Ben said, "Remember the '50s?"

"Sure."

"Those Reds of the '50s, they never won a World Series," Ben said. "They were before the Big Red Machine. Not a Bench, Perez or Rose in the bunch...not even an Eric Davis to bring it up closer. None of that glamour. Our boys were named Smoky Burgess, Ed Bailey, Ray Jablonski, Johnny Temple, Roy McMillan, and of course Ted Kluszewski, Gus Bell and Wally Post. Big Klu, Bell and Post, brother could they hit. Hit those 222 homers that year, 1955 I believe it was, those balls popping out of Crosley Field left and right. Klu was the lefty. Post was the righty. Tied the league record. Klu hit those clean line drives, like hanging rope, remember? Wally Post hit missiles. You had kids waiting outside the left field fence to catch him when he socked one. He once hit one over a building that was some four hundred feet away. They had no pitching, that's why they couldn't win. Big Klu made all the headlines, and deservedly so. One great year after another. He was up there with Mays, Snider, Banks, 40 homers that year, drove in more than 100 runs. But Wally Post, he was part Indian, I believe. He had those high cheekbones. A silent type of individual. Kept to himself. One great year, but what a year!

"To me, that's the greatest achievement of all. The rest of them were blessed. They had natural ability. To me that's no big deal. But to eke out one great year from minimum gifts, now that's something. That's all you can ask of a man, or a woman, to give you that one great year, don't you think? That was Wally Post. I'll never forget him. He came in here once, you know."

Ben began to reflect, lost himself in reverie. Now I never disbelieved him when he told people so-and-so had been here, and I never believed him, either. It was part of the atmosphere of Ben's News and Smoke Shop, that kind of talk. It was part of Ben. Made no difference to me if Wally Post had been here or not. Ben was here and that was enough.

But now he handed me the baseball and sure enough it was autographed, to Ben, by Wally Post.

"Keep it," he said.

Out of politeness, I declined.

He said he had only kept it around to remind him of the value of one great year, something we all had in us, and at his age, no, he didn't need it anymore. But maybe I did, he said, so I kept it, because maybe I did. Yes, maybe I did.

I found out something funny about myself. The only thing I looked forward to all day was going to Ben's. That was about all that got me up in the mornings. That being the case I decided to change my life swiftly and completely, and quit moping around. THERE IS NO MORE STEPHANIE.

I answered an ad for an advertising copywriter, since I had written much of Fat Jack's copy, not just the boiler room stuff, but stuff that also got into the papers. I'd have to brush up on my objectives, of course. I showed up on one of the top floors of the Carew Tower. I met a receptionist named Mary. Then I met a man named Mr. Snow. He was a short man and powerfully built and wore a crew cut. I had filled out an application form but neither Mary nor Mr. Snow seemed to care too much about that, as much as what kind of water I drank. When I said tap water Mary and Mr. Snow shared a knowing look and a smile.

"That's poison, you know," said Mr. Snow.

"Am I in the right place? I'm here about the copywriter's job."

"By all means," said Mr. Snow. "So let me show you a film."

Which was partly about all the chemicals Americans drank from tap water, and mostly about a new filtering system that got all that out.

Mr. Snow asked me how I felt about the presentation.

"Fine," I said. "Is that what I'd be advertising?"

"Why yes. That's the product. Do you think you could sell that product?"

"Of course."

"To your friends, relatives?"

I didn't get the connection, until it was explained that I first had to BUY one of these units.

"I thought I'd be writing copy."

"That, too."

"What sort of salary are we talking?"

"Salary? No salary. You keep ten percent of all the sales you make."

"Sales?"

"You'd be selling mostly to friends and relatives, using your home unit as a sample. But you have to BELIEVE in the product. Now, for this unit, your fee is a mere twelve hundred dollars..."

Crooks. They were crooks. They sold WATER! Like Morris Silver selling holes in the ground.

Which didn't mean that I didn't keep trying. I went out for interviews several times a week figuring it was time to find a job suitable for Stephanie, when we finally got together again, and I knew we would, at which time I'd be able to tell her that I was no longer LIMITED. Or maybe just telling her that I was off my can would be enough to make her happy.

Chapter 33

Her mother, as usual, answered the phone.

"I wish you would stop this," she said. "Have you spoken to your friend?"

"Yes, I've spoken to Maishe."

"Then he's told you."

"Everything."

"Then you know this family has suffered a great tragedy."

"I am part of that family, Mrs. Eaton."

"Eli, at a time like this we deserve our peace."

"I simply want to talk to her."

"I assure you that Stephanie will get the best medical treatment available. Maybe someday..."

"Now. Please."

"But Stephanie doesn't want to talk to you, Eli."

"There must be something..."

"There is NOTHING."

* * *

Mona was acting strange. I couldn't figure out what it was. She wasn't her usual friendly self and wasn't doing much talking, at least not to me. You get to know your people after a while and you get so you can tell one silence from another.

I figured she was upset over the dirty work she was now doing, known in the business as upscaling, which went like this: You called a person who had already purchased a medium-priced carpet and you acted ignorant. You said you had her order right in front of you, ready for delivery and installation, but weren't sure which carpet she had bought, due to an error on the part of the salesman. The order failed to specify. Had she bought the medium-priced carpet, or the more expensive one? The medium-priced, came the answer. Oh, you said. It's none of my business. I only work here in shipping. But, between you and me, the more expensive brand is quite a deal...resists stains and comes with not a 20, but a 30-year guarantee. So which one should we send out to you, Mrs. Blank?

The risk here was that it could all backfire, the customer might cancel the entire deal, even declining the medium-priced carpet she had already signed for, and that was one reason Mona hated upscaling; the other was that even though Mona could live with the marginal ethics of telephone soliciting, this was a step beyond, a leap from sales, and all the deceptions that involved, into the realm of outright crookedness.

Mona even had trouble verifying, the process by which you tested the strength of a lead by phoning the potential customer and never saying the obvious, which is, are you sure you want to buy? Most people said no, I just said yes to get the damned solicitor off the phone – or, no, I've changed my mind, or, no, I never agreed to anything. So what you said was, I'm just calling to check your address, Mrs. Blank, and if Mrs. Blank gave you her address that was a fairly strong lead, and if you said, fine, our representative will be over at the appointed time, and she still agreed, then you had a very strong lead.

But even that Mona considered deceptive, but manageable, to her conscience.

Upscaling was another story.

"You don't have to do it if you don't want to," I said.

She shrugged.

"What's the problem, Mona?"

She shrugged again.

"Out with it, Mona."

"I have news for you," she said.

I winced. You get so you dread news, even good news. My mom got that way toward the end and I noticed the same thing with many older people who'd been through a lot. They didn't want to hear news. Even good news.

"Stephanie called."

I looked at her.

"At least she said it was Stephanie."

I kept looking at her.

"But it sure didn't sound like Stephanie."

"What do you mean?"

"I mean it didn't sound like Stephanie."

But anyway, I was supposed to await her phone call and not, absolutely not try to get in touch with her. She'd get in touch with me. She had been very strict about that, according to Mona. Mona didn't know the story so it figured, her not understanding why Stephanie's voice had changed. She had probably been stabbed there.

So it was back to that, back to waiting. I waited the day, the night, another day another night, until the call finally came and it was Stephanie. It was Stephanie. I could hardly hear her – she sounded as though she were holding a hand over the mouthpiece, muffled.

But that was understandable. "Can you meet me?" she said without so much as a hello or a how-are-you.

Also understandable.

"Stephanie?"

"Can you meet me?"

"Where? When?"

She mentioned the deserted parking lot a couple of blocks from deserted Fleischman Park at a deserted hour, one a.m., all of which made sense for someone who did not want to be seen. Perfectly understandable. She didn't even want me to see her face. "You have to promise not to look at me," she said.

I was to stay in the parking lot, kill the lights, turn down the rearview mirror, wait for her to pull up, open the back door to let her in without looking at her, and we'd communicate that way, with her sitting in back, me in front, awkward of course, but understandable.

"I promise," I said.

She was adamant about my not setting eyes on her.

There was one more rule. If for some reason I couldn't make it, I was not to contact her at home.

Understandable. I knew the situation.

Chapter 34

Maishe said, "Something smells."

"What's wrong?"

He couldn't put his finger on it – except that it was SURPRISING.

"I mean, just like that – out of the blue."

I said most of my life was JUST LIKE THAT.

"Out of the blue?"

Most of his life was out of the blue.

"No," he said. "Most of life follows a pattern. This isn't Stephanie's pattern. All this...SCHEMING."

He suggested I drop the whole thing.

"Let's go to New York," he said.

"No."

"Look at you, Eli. YOU'RE stuck in a pattern."

Maishe said he was going to New York. With or without me.

Chapter 35

I waited. She couldn't have picked a more
desolate spot. Abandoned cars, tires, not even a
street light within four blocks. Avondale. Now a
ghetto. A bar two blocks away and even that was
abandoned. Finally, it wasn't the silver Jaguar X12
that pulled up, and this was understandable. In fact
the car was pretty beat up, whatever it was. But all
right.

She parked behind me. I watched her get out,
her face completely covered with a black and red
shawl. She halted when she noticed me staring so I
quickly turned my head, which prompted her to
move in and then enter the back seat in one athletic
leap. She fairly bolted in. I had the rearview mirror
turned down as she instructed. I felt her eyes watching me but the funny thing was, I didn't feel
Stephanie's eyes. They were someone else's eyes,
also understandable because Stephanie WAS someone
else.

Nothing was happening.

I was reluctant to speak; wrong choice of words might take her away, given how skittish she had become.

"Stephanie?" I said.

Still nothing. I started the car and slowly drove around the parking lot as if I were just trying to relax the two of us and casually passed by her car, about 30 feet away – but even from that distance and even in the dark it was unmistakable. Those were Kentucky license plates...

* * *

The Reds were doing all right and Dad saw that as a good sign. I stayed with him for a week and he never asked me what had happened. This thing about RANDOMNESS was more Dad's than Beckett's. Dad didn't ask questions. He expected anything to happen. I had been stabbed twice in the chest when I turned around. I lunged to intercept the knife but Sonja managed to get in two stabs amid a flurry of strikes. She was saying all sorts of things but I couldn't make out the language. Something about seeing people as they really were INSIDE, and that now it was my turn. She was very pissed off. So was I. Not at her coming at me with that knife and trying to cut the life out of me as much as having this person do all this, and consumed by all this, this hatred, for NO REASON – that I could think of. There probably were people who had a legitimate right to go after me with a knife and I would have been horrified all right, but not ticked off.

But this was annoying. That a STRANGER should have it in for you like this.

Hatred ought to be something you EARNED. Deserved. Just like love.

The randomness was what ticked me off.

But even randomness wasn't really random. It was systemized according to the law of averages, which had an order all its own. The more people you saw the more likely you were to run into one of every kind, and I had finally found my sickie, a woman who singled me out as her cause, her struggle, her kampf. How many girls had I interviewed for telephone solicitor? Hundreds. Among them came a Stephanie, and a Sonja. Law of averages.

After those couple of stabs – and I didn't know how seriously they had penetrated – we grappled until I overcame her and shoved her out of the car. She still held the knife. I punched her in the mouth, which prompted her to let go of the weapon. Then I had her by the neck and began tightening my grip. She managed to say: "Me too? Just like New York?"

So I let go.

"That bullpen," Dad said in admiration.

There were times when I could lose myself in a game and find myself living and dying with each ball and strike. But other times I'd find myself riveted to Dad's radio and then realize that five innings had gone by without my noticing. Two people who should have paid a price, gotten the CHAIR, the guy who

plotted Lou's death, and Sonja, the girl who had
ruined Stephanie – both were alive and well and
living in Cincinnati, including the wife-beating
neighbor upstairs and all the other wife-beaters and
child molesters. I couldn't figure it out. There was
no getting at them. The guy who had killed Lou
had committed the perfect crime because he had
committed no crime, technically. Sonja? Stephanie
would never testify against her and I was helpless to
bring her in on account of that thing in New York,
which would bring me in as well, if I were on the
books. I probably was. Maybe not. I just didn't know.

But it just didn't make sense, how things worked
out. I wondered how many other people had done all
sorts of things and were never punished and HELL,
that included me! Was that my punishment, to know
that among us walked evil – evil that was never
recompensed? You were brought up to believe that
good merits good and evil merits evil and you knew
more people were a shade off, when it came to the
good. But you never imagined that BLOODSHED, for
example, went unpunished. Made you think. Made
you wonder about what was around you. What
secrets people had.

To say that life was unfair, well, that was trite, of
course, but we were beyond that, into something
much darker, more than randomness, outright chaos
IF IN THE EYES OF JUSTICE THERE WAS NO
DIFFERENCE BETWEEN GOOD AND EVIL. Here on
earth, you mean, the good perish, evil prevails, and to
top it all off, there may not even be an afterlife! Then

what? Then those bumper stickers are correct: Life sucks and then you die.

Dad sat there in the big cushy chair glancing over his scorecard. The game was over. Always a letdown. There was comfort during the game. Kept you busy, even if you were diverted. Kept you serene knowing that something important was happening that wasn't really important. Win or lose he never said a word after the game. Took a shot of cognac and went straight to bed.

"Good night," he said.

"Good night, Dad."

Did he know that I'd been stabbed? Did he know I was his son? Probably not. I arrived straight from the hospital. He saw me. Made me a cup of tea. I often wondered if he knew I was his son. Not that I was complaining. It was better this way. I just wondered.

The injury hurt after the second day, when the sedation wore off. I felt myself burning up inside.

If I knew Sonja, she'd write it off as an accident – and maybe she was right.

Yeah. Everything was an accident. Really it was.

Chapter 36

I decided to write her a letter. In this age letter writing was a trifle more advanced than smoke signals – what with phones, faxes and e-mails – you never thought of taking pen in hand. As for me, I'd thought of every which way to reach her, even preparing to climb up the outside walls to her room, and until now it hadn't dawned on me to WRITE HER A LETTER.

My first letter was very long and very poetic and very romantic, and so touching; a regular Robert Browning. Our circumstances, come to think of it, weren't that much different. I even vowed to heal her with the abundance of my love. I even said it didn't matter how disfigured she was...

Fortunately I didn't mail it, nor the second, nor the third, fourth, fifth, sixth or seventh attempts. To tell a woman how you really felt...it just wasn't the American way. I certainly wasn't trained in that direction. I was never any good at whispering sweet nothings, especially when I didn't mean it, and now, from lack of exercise, even when I did. Everything came out so mushy you wanted to puke.

Maybe I inherited that from my father, that aloofness.

So I kept whittling away at this letter like that story about Fish Sold Here, where a man walks into the shop and says to the owner, "Why the word fish? Everybody knows they're fish." Agreed. "And why sold? Of course you're selling." Agreed. "And why Here? Where else?" Seeing the logic, the owner took the sign down.

I didn't reduce it that far, to obliteration, although I did think, I did assume that she knew my feelings for her. I shouldn't have to tell her. Except that I remembered her telling me that you can't assume, you must tell a woman. They're funny that way, even the beautiful ones – imagine, then, the ones damaged beyond recognition. But she ought to know that nothing so superficial could make a difference to me. I did not care how she looked.

The letter I finally sent said this:

Dear Stephanie:
    Cut the crap.
    Marry me.

Chapter 37

Harry's son-in-law, Stanley Blair, the accountant, was made vice-president, second in command, which dropped Fat Jack down a notch even though he was still manager – but now with almost no chance of taking over the business. Call it FAMILY. Call it POLITICS. That's the way it was, and I felt bad for Fat Jack, who was actually more family to Harry Himself than this stiff-necked, antiseptic, nose-to-the-figures, bottom-line-loving Stanley Blair. Fat Jack ran the place with a kind of bravado and flair and improvisation that was as out of style as the corner grocer. Harry Himself was now completely removed from store operations. He only came in so he wouldn't have to be home. Fat Jack had to get everything okayed by Stanley Blair.

Which he did, about one out of ten times. Nobody but nobody intimidated Fat Jack. This got him in hot water, as when he ran an Anniversary Sale and Stanley Blair, downstairs in the showroom, in front of everybody, asked him whose anniversary it was and Fat Jack said he didn't know, what's the difference?

"What's the DIFFERENCE?"

"All right. It's my wedding anniversary."

"Things are going to change around here."

That's where I came in after a week's absence, and it always seemed to be like that when you were gone and came back...things changed. Fat Jack whispered: "Better hurry on upstairs before he starts on you." Fat Jack wasn't the whispering kind, and not only that, but he seemed to be losing weight. Or maybe it was just his diminished status that made him appear thinner and less robust. Slim Jack? Skinny Jack? It just didn't go. Fat Jack or nothing.

Stanley Blair did start on me. Got himself an efficiency expert from Connecticut, very friendly jokey kind of guy, to take a look around the place, see where some chopping could be done, asking questions, only asking, no decisions being made, don't worry, nobody's getting fired, we're only doing this to promote efficiency and corporate EXCELLENCE, result being that half the salesmen were fired, first to go was Morris Silver, and Mona was not for long either, terrific person that she was, HEIRLOOM of the company that she was – but she wasn't CARRYING HER WEIGHT.

I handed in my resignation to Fat Jack. He refused to accept it – "Hang in," he said.

But he quit before I did.

"Who needs this bullshit?" he said. "I got money. Even if I didn't, who NEEDS THIS BULLSHIT?"

I asked to see Harry Himself and was given an audience. His office was the same as before. So was he. Only in addition to the feebleness I had detected earlier, this time he was also gloomy. He was a handsome man. Beautiful silver hair. Full face, dramatically lined. You expected him to roar – especially by reputation. But he spoke softly.

"Do you know what's going on?" I asked him.

"What's going on?"

"That guy is tearing this place apart."

He shrugged. "He's the boss."

"He is?"

"Yes he is, and he knows what he's doing."

"He does?"

"I'm sorry if you're unhappy."

"Everybody's unhappy. Fat Jack just QUIT!!"

"Stanley's my son-in-law."

"Fat Jack was your son, wasn't he?"

"Business is business."

Life goes on.

There was a part of him – I could see it in his eyes – that agreed with me. He had simply been swept away by the tide of everything that was TODAY. Automation. Bottom-line. Even the ethics had changed. The small larcenies, the little white lies, the wheeling and dealing, the handshake that was as good as a contract, the loyalties to the people who had come up with you that were the bedrock of the American retailer were things of the past. Harry Himself was a thing of the past. You couldn't feel sorry for him, of course. He had those millions stashed away. But maybe you felt sorry for the loss of the impromptu vigor that had created the Harry

Monocles. There were no more entrepreneurs. There were no more pioneers.

What we had now were the Stanley Blairs.

Stanley was astonished to learn that we were still operating out of a Criss-Cross Directory.

We were not using an updated DATABASE that more accurately PROFILED our prospects.

I had told him that zip codes were all we needed. Give me the zip code and I give you the person. As every direct marketing man knew, the zip code itself WAS the profile, told you not only where the person lived but how he lived, how much money he made, his religion, his hobbies, where he spent his money, on what he spent his money, and even his thoughts. As peripatetic as this nation was, people still lived among their own and if this was stereotyping, well then, yes, that's what it was. That's what it had to be if you didn't want to start selling refrigerators to the Eskimos or Oriental Rugs in Price Hill.

Stanley brought in a guy to computerize the boiler room, and by the way, no more boiler room. Stanley warned against using that term. This was TELEMARKETING. The room was refurbished, very attractively. New desks were brought in, a new air-conditioning unit was installed. Drapes were hung, the floors were carpeted.

All that for the computers. The people? Gone. The computers would now do the dialing and the soliciting.

No salesmen were allowed upstairs.

I was gone way before then.
Lou Emmett had died just in time.

Chapter 38

Three weeks after I sent the letter a silver Jaguar pulled up outside my apartment in Mount Adams. It was a Sunday. The summer heat had burned off to a fall chill. Early morning, the sun was shining, kids were outside riding their bikes.

I had shaved. I never shaved on Sundays but this Sunday I had as if in expectation.

She sat in the car. I waited for about 15 minutes. Then I stepped out. I was afraid she'd take off. But she didn't. She got out, straightened, put her arms around me and held me close, very close, and just held me like that, sobbing and holding and not letting go.

Then we walked in.

"I thought you'd be in New York by now," she said.

"Maishe told you?"

"He said you were both going to New York."

"Not me. Not until I heard from you."

"But he went, didn't he?"

"I guess he did. Never thought he would. But he did."

"Maybe you should have gone with him."

"No."

She laughed. "Some letter you wrote."

"Sorry. It was the best I could do."

Now she began crying again. "That was the most beautiful love letter any woman ever got. If you only knew what it did for me, Eli! It...it...it did everything. I've been in tears ever since."

"Well that's no good."

"Oh yes it is."

She had much on her mind, being cooped up like that all this time, and had really vowed never to show her face again – until that letter. I let her do most of the talking. Every few minutes she'd burst into tears. Mostly on account of the letter. She said nothing about suicide attempts. She said nothing about how it happened, how Sonja lured her, how Sonja attacked her. She did say she was a thoroughly changed person, and I could see that for myself. The original Stephanie never cried. The original Stephanie was never so forthright, so giving. She came plain out and said the only thing that kept her going was the hope that we'd get together, through the fear of how I'd react when I saw her, how terrifyingly ugly she'd become.

As she spoke she gazed at me boldly, unblinkingly, as if daring me to behold her new features.

I found myself turning away. It was involuntary. But I couldn't look at her. I couldn't. I just couldn't.

"We were like children," she said. "Playing games."

"We took turns."

"I was bad."

"But when you were good…"

We both laughed.

Silence.

"I guess some good came of it," she said.

"Like what?"

"I've come to appreciate…certain things. You realize, of course, I'll always be confined."

"You mean you'll never leave the house?"

"Eli – LOOK AT ME!"

Up to then we had been rolling along.

"I'm looking."

"No you're not. Eli, when I look in the mirror I wish I were dead."

I tried a joke. "So don't look in the mirror."

"But you would have to look at me, if you meant what you said."

What had I said?

"Do you remember what you said?"

I wasn't playing dumb.

"In the letter. MARRY ME, you said. Do you still want to marry me?"

"Yes I do."

I didn't say it with much conviction because I didn't know how I felt, or maybe I did and didn't like what I was feeling. I was tired. Suddenly I was tired. I just wanted to go to sleep. I knew it wouldn't be easy but I never thought it would be as tough as this. It wasn't tough, it was impossible. There wasn't even a vestige of her original self, not even a hint of the Stephanie that I had loved, adored. I tried to conjure her up as she had been that first day, the day of the interview, and it did come to me but quickly faded as the shadow of a passing bird.

She gathered up her purse and walked to the door.

"I do love you," I said, as something from memory.

"I knew it would be like this," she said, walking back.

I found my mind drifting. I wanted to watch a ballgame. There was a game on this afternoon and I had been looking forward to it, pointing to it, as I'd been doing ever since I left Harry's Carpet City and discovered all this free time, with nothing to point to, except the ballgames.

I didn't want to get her out of my apartment as much as I wanted to get myself the hell out. I wanted to breathe some air. Go to New York. Be with Maishe. Be with anybody else. The walls were closing in. Stephanie was closing in. Stephanie? This was Stephanie?

THIS WAS STEPHANIE?

"I don't know what more I can say," I said.

"I know you Eli. I know you're trying. I expected you to try. But I'm not your rich beautiful girl anymore."

I shrugged.

"Am I? Oh I'm still rich..."

"You're still..."

I was about to say "beautiful" but she wasn't stupid. No, she was very smart.

Maishe had told me to live with the dream. If I had been smart that would have been enough.

I should have gone with him to New York. Forget Cincinnati. Forget Stephanie.

Now I couldn't forget.

I'd always remember this.

"I'll always love you," she said.

If there was one thing I couldn't stand it was lines like that.

"I'm leaving," she said.

I couldn't wait.

"Don't," I said.

"But you want me to."

I was feeling very sleepy again. I wanted to get under the covers and go to sleep. I always put myself to sleep by dreaming about Stephanie. Now what? Could I erase what I had just seen and if I could, what would I use to replace her? There had been nobody even close.

"Stay as long as you want."

She chuckled. "Have I changed that much? You can't wait to get rid of me. Eli..."

"I guess I'm just tired."

You imagine the dramatic moments of your life, none as sweet as the reunion with an old flame, and does it ever turn out according to plan? Like in the movies? Never. This? This was the biggest failure of all. A flop.

"So will you be going to New York?"

"I don't know. I guess. I don't know."

"You don't have a job."

"I know."

"I can't believe they let Fat Jack go. I liked him so much."

"It was just a job."

"That's where we met."

She didn't say that sentimentally. She wasn't being sentimental at all. Just stating facts. Reviewing our past. Something you tended to do when you knew there'd be no future. Every now and then there'd be a glimmer of the old Stephanie, the headstrong, self-assured Stephanie, aglow from the fullness of youth, wealth and beauty. But it was only a flicker, in her eyes, if you caught it in time, a flicker, no flame.

You tried to conjure up the magic that had been, force it through.

"I think you ought to know why I've rejected plastic surgery. It was explained to me that my face would be pulled in so many different directions that after a while, perhaps five years, it would all cave in, and be even worse than it is now. That was my choice, Eli. In case you were wondering."

"No I wasn't."

"I've seen people with plastic surgery..."

"So have I."

"Looks wonderful the first year..."

"I don't blame you. You made the right decision."

Her lower lip began to quiver. "Would it be asking too much...I mean you're being so...unemotional."

"You know I don't cry."

"But detached?"

"I'm not detached."

"Would it be asking too much...for you...before I go...to make love to me?"

I said nothing.

"You know I'm still a virgin."

"No, I didn't know."

"You thought I lost it in California."

"I did."

"Well I didn't. I was saving it for you. Sounds silly, doesn't it?"

"Sounds nice."

"I mean that ANY woman would save herself...I mean that's so old-fashioned."

"But nothing to regret."

"Oh? I don't know about that."

"You think you're missing that much?"

"I don't know. That's the point. Am I?"

"I don't think so. Sex is the most overrated thing."

"And you would know, wouldn't you."

"It's no great thing, Stephanie. It's all Hollywood."

"Has it occurred to you that I may never know what it's like?"

"But I just told you what it's like."

She laughed. "You're being funny. You're still funny. That guy in California meant nothing to me, you know. I guess I was just trying to make you jealous. I was trying to hurt you. There's never been anyone but you, Eli."

"Same here."

"But not anymore. Is that right?"

"I didn't say that."

"No, but you're not saying anything else, either. You're being very distant."

"Detached, right?"

"How can I make you love me again?"

Maybe it was a bit melodramatic but it was the heart of the matter, a question I'd been asking myself from the minute I caught my first glimpse of her today. How could I love her again? Would I have to MAKE myself love her? You couldn't FORCE yourself to love somebody, could you? If I didn't love her anymore, what kind of person was I? Hadn't I said that looks meant nothing to me? Especially where she was concerned?

But there it was. No truth about her. But a truth about me.

Sonja had shown the inside of ME.

That's whom she exposed.

She knew her work, Sonja did. She wasn't crazy at all. She was a pro.

Hadn't she been right when she said there were worse things than death?

Had she killed Stephanie it would have been a FAVOR.

She was no nut, Sonja. She was smarter than all the rest of us. All the nuts were.

"I wish you'd say something," Stephanie said.

If there was one thing I was starting to resent it was conversation. Talk, talk, talk. Especially conversations like this, when all you were doing was giving out lines, since everything was understood. She understood exactly how I felt and vice versa, so why talk? If it were up to me people would stop talk-ing altogether. There was nothing to say anymore. You'd think after thousands of years here on earth we'd have it all straightened out by now.

"We used to have such lovely conversations," she said. "Can I expect even that much?"

"Always."

"But nothing more?"

She wasn't being weepy. Very straightforward.

"To be honest," I said... "to be honest..."

"Yes, please, let's be honest."

"It's been a shock," I said.

"You think I don't know that, Eli? You think I haven't rehearsed this a thousand times in my mind? Do you know what it took to get me to come here? I knew precisely how you'd react. Thankfully, you spared me all the usual sentiments. For that I'm grateful. I knew you would spare me the pity and any phony declarations of undying love. You came through on that, but all this reserve...I guess I was hoping...hoping you'd see me as I used to be. I guess I was hoping you'd see me as WE used to be. I guess I was hoping...oh, Eli. Eli."

I stuffed tobacco in my pipe and lit up and stretched my legs.

"I was thinking you'd get used to this," she said, pointing to her face. "In time."

She said if I insisted that she'd undergo plastic surgery, restoration they called it, she'd do it, for me.

"No," I said.

"No what?"

243

"You're fine the way you are."

She chuckled.

"So what do you want me to do?"

"I don't know."

"You mean there's nothing left."

"I didn't say that," I said.

"Are you angry?"

"Yes."

"At me?"

"Of course not. At...everything."

"Well I'm not angry anymore. I've gotten over the anger."

"I know. But I haven't."

"It's too late to be angry," she said.

"I'll get over it, I'm sure."

She laughed. "Aren't we something. Always something coming between us. As though fate...and who would have thought of this? Mind if I stay the afternoon? I'll just stay here quietly and watch the ballgame with you."

Which she did, and it was very peaceful. We didn't talk much. Just sat and watched the ballgame, and I WAS starting to get used to her and remember her. I thought of the many times before when I would have given my life just to spend such a peaceful afternoon together. It never worked out when she was the vivacious highflying Stephanie. We were always performing for one another, jousting, taking turns at being cool. But now it was peaceful between us. The heat was gone. I had meant it when I had said we were in love TOO MUCH. Yes there was such a thing as too much. It got to be overwhelming. We couldn't handle it or at least I certainly couldn't. Now it was different, now that we were brought down, both brought down by the same thing. Loving her had been the same as pain, hurting all the time. I had wondered how it would end, the pain. I always wondered how it would end.

At night we sent out for pizza. The delivery boy gave her a double-take. I tried not to notice.

Why had she shown herself to him?

She said she did it on purpose, to show me the worst of what would be in store. "For a lifetime," she said.

After we ate pizza I fell asleep on the couch. I felt her put a cover over me before I drifted off. I got up several hours later and she was gone.

I felt empty. I felt sad and sick and empty.

Then I looked outside. It was dark. Her car was still there. I walked out into the hallway and she was standing there, shivering. I put my arms around her and held her for a very long time. Then I brought her inside and took her clothes off.

We made love.

Before she drifted off she said it was the first time she felt sleepy ever since it happened.

"Shh," I said and stroked her hair.

I watched her sleep, so peaceful.

I figured never mind this lifetime business. One great year. Maybe together we had that one great year ahead of us.